HOOF BEATS

.

by

Rae D'Arcy

Note for Librarians: A cataloguing record for this book is available from Library and Archives Canada at www.collectionscanada.ca/amicus/index-e.html

Printed in Victoria, BC, Canada.

ISBN: 978-1-4251-8647-0 (sc)

Our mission is to efficiently provide the world's finest, most comprehensive book publishing service, enabling every author to experience success. To find out how to publish your book, your way, and have it available worldwide, visit us online at www.trafford.com/10510

Trafford rev. 8/5/2009

www.trafford.com

North America & international
toll-free: 1 888 232 4444 (USA & Canada)
phone: 250 383 6864 ♦ fax: 250 383 6804

Thanks to Arielle for being my reader
and to Charity for her encouragement.

Chapter 1

My earliest memory is of hoof beats. I'm surrounded by darkness. It's warm and moist. And there is the steady sound of hoof beats.

My mother told me she rode horse back on her big, roman-nosed, Missouri Fox Trotter named Gustavo, right up until the day before she delivered. Gus' racking gait was so smooth, mom said it never jolted her, or me inside her.

When I mentioned I had intrauterine memories of his hoof beats, Mom just scoffed. "What about the black, moist environment?" I asked.

"Gus was black. As soon as we got home from the hospital, I took you down to the pasture to meet him. He stuck his nose right in your face and blew. I'm sure that was the moisture. I laid you on his back. He looked round at you and then walked all the way to the barn. You were awake the whole time; your face against his sun warmed back and your tiny fingers tangled in his mane.

"Every morning when I went down to the barn, you went along in your carrier. I set you right in front of Gus in the cross ties. He'd whicker softly and you'd laugh. His forelock would tickle your face. Your little hands would be in fists and bouncing around. Sometimes it looked like you were using his nose as a punching bag but he never minded. Even when you got hold of his nostrils he just blew in your face until I pried your fingers off. Then I'd put you in a carry pack facing forward and mount up. By the time you were eighteen months, I could tell you were balancing yourself. By two years, you were sitting astride on your own. For your third birthday I got you your own horse."

"Yes. I remember Bo Diddly. I remember the lessons with Miss Mason, too."

"She was far too easy on you."

I looked at my mother's wrinkled face. Even prostrate in bed surrounded with the faint odor of bed pan, layered with the aseptic smell of medicines and ointments, she still had that look of superiority about her with her nose in the air. I felt that dislike ballooning inside of me, crowding heart and lungs. I couldn't breath. My heart constricted. I wanted to love her. Especially at this last moment.

She was tiring; her breath starting to come in wheezes; her eyes shut as she barely whispered, "You could still become a highly competitive rider if you'd lose some weight and apply yourself."

I replied nothing to that remark. She had always let me know where I lacked; made me feel it was a personal affront to have let her down.

She gave a small gasp. With a pause between each word, she said, "I'm... so... afraid."

"Mom, you've had such a full storybook life."

"Have I? I was never good enough to compete with the likes of Jennifer Cramer, Carley Carlyle, or the Simmons twins; not rich enough to have the best horses. Madison, promise me you'll marry money. Life is so much easier with money. I so want you to be happy."

It struck me at that moment that she had wanted me to succeed where she felt she had not. She wanted me to be happy fulfilling her dreams, not my own. I had her love of horses, just not the same desire to compete in the high echelon of elite equestrian events. The expensive, talented horses she had bought were wasted on me. Although I appreciated and enjoyed the athletic horses, I thought I would have been just as happy on a backyard horse.

I moved closer to her and took her fragile hand in mine. The skin was thin and delicate; the fingers long and elegant. They should have graced a piano. Instead, they had groomed dirty, sweat-covered horses, guided soft-mouthed mounts through three-day eventing courses. She had put me on a horse before I was born and three days afterwards. I could love her for that.

Her eyes were shifting as though she was a novice searching for dressage letters, and her breath was becoming ragged. "Madison?" It sounded like a sob.

"I'm right here, Mom." I put my hands on either side of her face, leaned forward and kissed her forehead. "I love you, Mom."

I heard a long exhale and then she went still. I was surprised that the tears came so readily to my eyes. I looked up at the ceiling thinking to see her spirit hovering. If it was there, it didn't choose to let me know. That was so like my mother.

Chapter 2

Mom died while I was on summer break between college and veterinarian school. Her timing, as always, was impeccable. She had been continuously attentive to my progress, purchasing new horses, engaging new trainers or instructors at precisely the right moment to keep my equestrian skills improving. She never insighted rebellion in me by selling the mounts I came to love, but kept them as schooling horses and started the Kurt's Equestrian Center. I even started earning money as I entered high school by giving beginner lessons. I really enjoyed that.

Pulling in the drive to Kurt's Equestrian Center following the other cars after mom's funeral, it finally hit me that some major changes needed to be made. I hadn't really paid attention to expressions on the faces of those attending. My mind was swirling around what course, of the many available, I was going to pursue. It now seeped into my awareness that there hadn't been many tears. The comments were, "She really knew how to get the best from her horses and students," "She was a determined competitor," "She was extremely competitive."

Yep. That was mom. Now as I entered the house I grew up in, I realized her death closed a chapter of family dynamics and opened another. The scowl on Aunt Gwen's face and the stone-like expressions on Cousin Jan and her husband, Rick, testified to their own determination.

I had a bit of worry of my own. I needed to make some decisions. I wasn't ready to abdicate without thinking through my options, however.

I gave Aunt Gwen and Uncle Sam a kiss, walked past whirring air conditioners and the tables of food supplied by their church ladies to say hi to cousins Jan and Rick. They had been at the funeral. Why did I need to say "hi"? Was I trying to bridge the widening gap I felt between us?

I heard people reminiscing about a spectacular jump one of mom's horses had taken that everyone had thought was beyond the horse's capability. In fact, they had all resented her entering the class they thought was beyond them as a team.

"It was like she flew over the jump, grasped the horse with her knees and took him along."

"I remember that horse. Rockin Robin was its name. A bright red bay. Remember the shocked silence? Everyone was holding their breath and two seconds after they land the collective audience finally exhale and explode into clapping, whistles and cheers. They still had three jumps to go. The commotion startled the horse, but she got him focused in time to take those last three cleanly."

I had never heard that story before. It made me want to hear more stories of what my mom was like before I came along late in her life to end her eventing career. When the group turned their conversation to competitors in their own families, I moved on to another group. I wanted to be a fly on the wall. A couple ladies mom and Aunt Gwen's age were discussing how mercilessly she goaded me in my riding career. I already knew that; didn't need to hear it from others. I moved on. A couple middle aged women complained how mom drove their daughters to tears when she went to instructing.

I was tired of being the fly. My heart ached. I wasn't sure for whom; myself, those girls driven to tears when they probably just wanted to enjoy their horses, or my mom receiving such harsh criticism for trying to instill excellence. And then I heard hoof beats. I was on the right side of the house facing the pastures. The big boys were running, kicking up their heels in the sheer joy of being equines. The mares in the next field threw up their heads at the ruckus the geldings were making, paused with grass sticking out the sides of their mouths and then dropped them for another bite deciding such egocentricity wasn't worth watching.

The thundering hooves got my heart racing, though. I slipped into my room, changed into riding breeches and paddock boots, grabbed my riding helmet, and rushed out the back door toward the barns. The sun was warm on my face. The scent of freshly mowed grass filled my nose. I passed the flower garden and smelled hydrangea and roses. My favorite aromas, however, were in the barn; the perfumes of sage green, leafy, grass hay; various grains, and yellow, oat straw assailed my senses, set my nerves to tingling and put a smile on my face.

A car pulled into the parking lot. A girl got out wearing a smile as big as mine.

"Coming to ride, Erin?"

"Yes."

"How are the lessons coming?"

"Great. Chatty Cathy is a great horse to learn on."

"Are you looking forward to getting your own horse?"

The smile dimmed. "I don't think that will happen for a very long time."

"Well, it will give you something to look forward to."

We got our leads and headed for the pastures; she to the mares, I to the geldings who had calmed down and were gathered about the water trough. I was almost overwhelmed with a mixture of gratitude that horses had always been a part of my life, and sadness that so many people, young and old, struggled to keep one. And still others, no matter how much they longed for a horse, would never know that joy.

The stable hands worked around Erin and me as we groomed our mounts. Chatty Cathy didn't need as much primping as did Fritz, my sixteen, two high Hanoverian. He looked like he had been bajaing in the hills. By the time I had him spiffed up, pulled his legs to stretch the muscles and got into the arena, Erin and Chatty Cathy had worked up a sweat. We were out of the sun but there wasn't much of a breeze entering through the huge doors pushed all the way open on their tracks.

As Fritz's long stride moved us around the arena, I watched Erin maneuver Chatty Cathy through dressage tests. Erin had a knack for riding. You could tell she worked hard at her horsemanship. She was gentle with the mare that was past her prime but was giving her best. It wasn't everyone who could elicit that respect from the schooling horse. Chatty Cathy had been known to dump several students for rough hands or inattention.

Erin guided the mare into another arena to try jumps. Fritz and I did some collection, and ten and fifteen meter circles as warm up then went into the jumping arena. I was a bit nervous about Erin working in there alone. I needn't have worried. Erin was sticking to two foot jumps and as I went around the far end I saw one of the stable hands in the judge's box watching like a swim guard. I was pleased that Jan and Rick had kept that idea of mom's; that no one should ride without someone present in case of an emergency. I settled into enjoying my horse. We weren't preparing for a show. We were just having a good time.

This would be such a satisfying life, I thought, as Fritz cantered around the arena and pricked his ears even at the lowliest of jumps. And it's all set up and ready to go rather than another 4 years of veterinarian school. I wasn't a great student. I had to work hard to keep the grades up.

Then the guilt set in. That's exactly what Jan and Rick expected me to do; yank this place out from under them. They had done a good job of building up clientele and running it efficiently after mom was too ill to do it. It was providing them with a good income beyond what they paid as a franchise fee to mom, and the percentage they were required to put back into the business. I recollected the strained faces as they waited for me to make up my mind.

Mom's will left the entire estate, including the Kurt's Equestrian Center to me to do with as I chose. Oh, the temptation to give in to immediate gratification; quit school, help other people learn to ride the beautiful animals that made life grand. Maybe I'd even compete at a higher level, representing the royal blue/cadet blue of the Center, of course.

The sun was beginning to near the tree tops at the west edge of the pastures coating them in a gold glaze. We walked the cooled horses to the stables. People were beginning to trickle out of the house. I felt a twinge of guilt but then smiled, knowing mom would have approved. She hadn't been too concerned with what people thought of her. She knew what made her happy.

A chunky girl in royal blue denim jeans and cadet blue polo shirt approached. "Shall I put Fritz up for you, Madison?"

"No thanks, Shelly. Maybe another day."

"Want me to massage him after you groom?"

After a moment's hesitation, I said, "Sure. He'd like that." I had been about to refuse the offer but Shelly was an awesome groom; a conscientious and energetic worker. I thought she would love to have a horse of her own but she seemed satisfied exercising and caring for the schooling horses that were not being used at any particular time. I had taught her myself how to massage. She was good at it. I wasn't sure what aspirations she had. I often saw her watching instructors and trainers doing their thing. She soaked up all the information and then tried it on the horses she was exercising or on herself to improve her own riding. Was she satisfied just having access to all these horses that belonged to someone else at no expense for her? Did she think she had a good deal or was she just biding her time?

It reminded me of the first pro bono lessons I gave. Mom screamed that you didn't run a business by giving your product away. But dad gave me a wink and an approving nod on the sly, as I told her I'd make the girl work for them. It turned out to be more work than I expected but also more gratifying than I expected.

Between studying, riding, barn work and giving lessons, I didn't have much extra time for spending nights at a friend's house or an evening at a party. I still had friends, however, to sit with at lunch or pass notes to in study hall.

There was a thickset girl in our grade that was always reading horse novels like King of the Wind, Black Gold, and the Black Stallion series. I never really noticed her except for what horsey book she was reading again and yet again.

One day in the lunch room my friends were giggling as I took my seat next to them. I thought it was about the poor excuse for food on our trays and the heavy smell of fish sticks which was typical for Friday. But they pointed out that Melissa Johnson was reading My Friend Flicka for the gazillionth time since sixth grade. I knew that was true. I'd noticed the thread-bare hard back with yellowed pages on top the stack of books she carried from room to room and read during study hall instead of doing her home work or whispering to a neighbor.

When my friends were ready to leave, I told them I'd catch up with them. I went over to Melissa, tapped the book and said, "Flicka again? Don't you know it by heart?"

"What do you care?" It came out in a snarl. She rolled her eyes up to see who had been so rude as to invade her space. She rolled them back down to the page but they didn't move from side to side so she wasn't reading.

I sat down anyway. "I liked it too. Read it at least four times in sixth and seventh grades. But wouldn't you like something new? Maybe a bit more adult?"

"I've scoured the library for books like that. Haven't found any."

"You're right. It is slim pickings there. You need to go to the Book Nook. They have one titled A Passion for Horses. They're true horse stories. Or join a horse lover's book club. But most of those books are about caring for and training horses."

"Where do you find a book club?"

"Usually in horse magazines. Look for them in the magazine section at grocery stores or department stores. The Book Nook has the magazines, too."

With her eyes still on the page in front of her, she said, "Thanks, I will."

"So, do you ride?" It was a dumb question. I knew she didn't. She looked at me then with brown eyes full of longing and I was sorry I asked.

"No, do you?"

"Yeah. Well, gotta go. Look for that book or the magazines."

I scurried away without looking back. I knew the next words out of her mouth were going to be a request to ride my horse. I could have deflected by suggesting riding lessons but I had the feeling her parents, couldn't afford lessons.

I had the very book I was suggesting to her but I was possessive and wanted it to remain in good shape. I wasn't sure how well she'd take care of it. I didn't mind trying to broaden her horizons a bit, but I wasn't sure I wanted to be her friend. I guess I was afraid she'd grab me like a drowning person and pull me under. Better to just call encouragement from the shore.

I steered clear of her for several days, not even passing her in the lunch room. A couple weeks later I was using that time to cram for a chemistry test while feeding bland meatloaf into my mouth. She shoved a copy of A Passion for Horses between me and my textbook.

"I got it. Cost me twenty-five dollars."

I looked up. "Have you read it yet?"

"Of course. Twice."

"Time to get another one."

Her smile faded. "They're so expensive. Took me two babysitting jobs to get this one."

"Was it worth it?"

"I guess."

"Why not get some magazines and read real taking care of horses stuff?"

"It's hard work saving the money."

"Horses are hard work. If you can't work to save for a book, I doubt you could handle work around horses."

"I doubt I'll ever have a horse, anyway."

"Well, what about when you're out of school and have your own job? Maybe you could afford one then. Now you should be learning all you can in case that happens. Then you'll be better prepared to take on its care."

"That's so far away." After a pause she added, "How much are riding lessons?"

"Twenty-five dollars for group and thirty for private."

Melissa let out a long sigh.

"How bad do you want those lessons?"

"Pretty bad."

"Are you sure you don't just like the fantasy?"

"I don't know."

"Well, you think about it. If you really want to learn to ride and are willing to work to get them, maybe we can arrange something. I've got to go."

For about a week it seemed Melissa was avoiding me. I'd see her and she'd drop her eyes and go in a different direction. I figured she was embarrassed to tell me she didn't really want lessons, but finally there she was.

"I'd like to try to learn to ride. I'm still not sure if it isn't just a fantasy, but Mom said if I don't try it, I'll never know. And I'll only be able to take one lesson a month. It'll take me about that long to save for each lesson."

"You can work off the lesson."

"Doing what?"

"Mucking stalls, grooming horses, cleaning out feed pans and water buckets."

Melissa's eyes widened and her mouth tensed into a straight line.

"I'll teach you how. You learn it just like you learn anything else, Melissa."

"When do I start?"

She came before school. I started her out cleaning feed pans and water buckets. After a week she got to sit on a horse, holding imaginary reins. A stable hand led the horse around the arena while I watched and called corrections in how she was sitting and using her muscles. Her face gradually lost its tightness and sprouted a smile by the time she left, listing from side to side to accommodate sore thighs. I was pleased that she quickly showed initiative by getting right to work when she arrived in the mornings, and then asked for more work. Martin showed her how to clean a stall.

Because of her weight, she didn't mount very gracefully. She literally had to grasp pommel and cantle of the saddle, pull herself up leaning too far over the horse until she could get a leg over and then right herself and plop down into the saddle causing the horse's back to give a bounce. Still I gave the same instructions at the beginning of each session. "Foot in stirrup. Rise on that leg until it is straight. Swing other leg over horse aiming the foot into the stirrup on the far side. Sit gently onto the horses back."

She progressed from in hand riding to circles on a lunge line, and then on a lunge line for security but with real reins and guiding the horse this way and that herself. Like most students she had a hard time realizing you didn't use a pull on the reins to turn the horse. But by leg positions, shifting her weight on her seat bones, and simple squeezing of the reins she could tell the horse what she wanted.

She caught on, however, and by the time she took on brushing, picking hooves, bathing, pulling and braiding manes, she had cut the lunge line umbilical cord and was working in fifteen and twenty meter circles, serpentines, zigzags, and posting the trot.

She was putting in long days on the weekends and every holiday from school, earning enough for two lessons a week which she took after school during the week and thriving on the same barn aromas that gave me sustenance.

After Christmas she showed up with her own riding helmet and wearing tan riding breeches, paddock boots and half chaps. They were, no doubt, Christmas presents and not cheap ones at that. Someone at home believed in her interest in riding. Dressed in her new outfit, I was surprised to notice she had lost a considerable amount of weight and was mounting much more gracefully.

At school she never imposed if I was with other people but would wave and smile if I was alone. I was starting to respect her. I noticed she used study halls to get her homework done. Horse Illustrated and Equus took the place of the juvenile novels.

For the rest of our sophomore year and through our senior year, Melissa never missed a morning or weekend of work, or her two lessons a week. She was showing in dressage and arena jumping, and bringing home some ribbons on one of our lesson horses which was a great advertisement for our Center. But college loomed on both our horizons and redirected our lives. We lost touch.

Chapter 3

Everyone had stayed over at the ranch house I had grown up in. Even though Jan and Rick had lived in it the past four years, I still had a room here for when I was home on break, a job giving lessons to holiday students, and Fritz had a stall. When I came out of my room in the morning, I was a bit ashamed that I had kept them hanging for so long but I still wasn't sure what I wanted to do. Over and over in my mind played my options of shoulds, coulds, and wannas.

Aunt Gwen and Uncle Sam sat grim faced at the breakfast table. Uncle Sam was sopping up the last of an egg yolk with a piece of toast. Aunt Gwen had both hands around a steaming cup of black coffee. The smell of bacon and coffee filled the air and gave me a feeling of being home. I smiled and said "Good morning."

No one answered. The toaster popped up golden slices of bread. Orange juice gurgled into four ounce glasses. Jan and Rick carried their plates to the table. They both took big bites and chewed silently. I was beginning to feel a chill. I got a cup of coffee, added some sugar and sat at the table suddenly feeling like an intruder.

"Are you interested in continuing to run the center?" I asked getting right to the point.

"Only if it's ours. We aren't paying the ridiculous franchise fee and we'll decide how much to put back into the business."

I was taken aback by the angry tone of the voice. No one had looked at me. I wasn't even sure who had spoken as the flow of food around the tongue impeded a clear identification, although the emphasis on ONLY and OURS was plain enough.

"Are you saying you want to buy it?"

"At a reasonable price."

"Can Fritz stay here while I'm at school?"

"If you pay the boarding fee. It won't be your home anymore either."

I could feel the anger rising in my chest. They had lived here for free. Even with paying the franchise fee and the percentage of the gross income that had to be put back into the business, they had made big money. The schooling horses were already in the stalls and the clientele established when mom passed the reins to them five years ago. Had this animosity always been so obvious? Was I so wrapped up in my own affairs I hadn't noticed, or had they hid it until now?

Mom had wanted me to own, operate and show Kurt's Equine Center. Did I want to be a vet just to spite her? I certainly enjoyed the center but I knew I had a weakness for giving away lessons or bartering for barn work. Would I ruin the center financially?

As I looked at the faces around the table, all eyes averted, I felt a need to hear the steady hoof beats of Fritz. I knew he'd calm my nerves.

"If you'll excuse me. I thought I was ready for this conversation but I'll have to think on it a bit."

My chair scraped against the floor like fingernails on a chalk board. Their silence resounded like a slap in the face. The stable was abuzz with early morning chores. The horses had finished their breakfast and stood at the stall guards waiting expectantly. The privately owned horses would be heading for the pastures. Those used for lessons were put in the paddocks close by. The temperature was already heating up. I usually rode before ten o'clock, before the noon heat made it unbearable.

Several stable hands said good morning to me. Jake saw me coming and brought Fritz out to the cross ties. The horse already gleamed from a good grooming.

"Thanks Jake."

"No problem. I'll get your saddle."

I stood forehead to forehead with my friend inhaling his horsey aroma. "Fritz, what should I do? If I sell to Jan and Rick, where will I put you until I get through school? I can't stand the thought of selling you. For that matter, I almost can't stand the thought of not riding you while I'm in school. Maybe I shouldn't go to school."

"Of course you should, Madison," interjected Jake coming up behind me. "Why wouldn't you?"

"I can't keep this place and go to school too. When will I have time to ride Fritz? Not to show would be a waste of his potential. Say, you could run this place for me so I don't have to sell."

"I'd love to Madison, but the timing isn't right. We both need to think delayed gratification; long term goals." He was tacking up Fritz for me. The horse's head was already up; ears pricked in anticipation. "Running this place is a full time job. I'm going to school right now, too. Got to finish that first."

"I almost can't stand the thought of leaving this place."

"But you've done it for four years already."

"Because I knew I'd be back at the end of each semester. They've made it clear; they want me out of here. I love working with the horses and giving lessons."

"You can come back to it, Madison. Get your schooling first. I've seen how you give lessons without charging for them. My niece got to experience horses because of you."

"Who's your niece?"

"Brandi Andrews."

"Oh my gosh. How is she doing?"

"Great. Taking home lots of ribbons for Windhaven stable."

"I guess that means she doesn't take lessons here anymore then?"

"No. Jan and Rick don't do pro bono. She's doing barn work over at Windhaven. She's a hard worker. Chelsea really likes her work."

"Chelsea Bass is a great teacher, too."

"My brother-in-law is looking for a horse for Brandi."

I paused. "You want Fritz. Don't you think he's too much horse for Brandi?"

"Not by much. He's the next logical mount for her. He'd really help Brandi progress. He's a sweet horse; well mannered. Brandi would love him. He'd have a great home while you're off to school. You can visit and ride him anytime you'd want."

"If Brandi is working off lessons how would they pay the price of Fritz?"

"Grandpa has offered to loan enough to purchase Brandi an eventing horse; interest free."

"Why Fritz?"

"I've worked around him. I know him. I can vouch for his reliability. Actually, they'd be a perfect match. He has a lot to teach her. I'm sure he could take her to the nationals. Maybe internationals."

He paused. "And I've heard the gossip around the barn. You're going to need a place for him while you're at school. Sell the place to them, Madison. Sell Fritz so he doesn't go to seed. Leave the past behind. Bank the money so you can start over when you get out of school."

"You make it sound so right."

Jake grinned. "Come on. Leg up."

Brandi came the next day to show me her riding skills. I wasn't in a very good mood as I'd let Jan and Rick know I'd sell the Center to them. They haggled about the price. It was bad enough having to sell, and then they weren't lenient in any way as far as guaranteeing me a summer teaching job, and of course a stall for Fritz was out of the question. The sale would be a total break from my past. It was hurting already. To top it off, what sounded so right yesterday from Jake's mouth now felt like being taken advantage of because I was in a quandary.

It was a beautiful summer day; hot but with a breeze. I tried to respond to the hug Brandi gave me but this was just another person that was going to take something I loved away from me after I had graciously given her pro bono lessons to get her started in the life she was now loving. Still, I had to admit, Brandi had grown into quite a lovely, confident young woman. I had seen horses do that for young girls over and over again. Now, I watched as she handled Fritz superbly. I could see her potential as an equestrian and Fritz would indeed help her reach that potential. I could already see him giving her added confidence to stretch her abilities. And I had had a hand in creating this monster who was about to take away the only love of my life.

"I see what you mean, Jake." My voice cracked despite my efforts to keep calm.

Jake looked at me with concern but was all smiles as Brandi brought Fritz next to us. I reached up to stroke his muscular neck. My heart ached.

"What do you think, Brandi?" asked Jake. "Is he the horse of your dreams?"

Brandi looked down at me with a smile that resembled Jake's. "He is so awesome, Madison. I know it must be killing you to let him go. I promise to take good care of him. If it isn't too painful, you're welcome to come visit and ride him whenever you want."

I didn't want to look up at her. My tears blurred Fritz's bay coat. I felt Jake's hand on my shoulder and Brandi's gloved hand covered mine on Fritz's crest. I heard her sob, "I promise."

Over the next days, I busied myself about the barn, helping with the dirtiest work I could find: sweeping out dust webs, mucking stalls, cleaning tack, grooming. Fritz was shipped to Windhaven. Jan and Rick said I could finish the summer working there but I wanted gone. I put the money from the sale of the Center and Fritz into a CD account that was earning good interest and started packing my things. There were a few things I'd take along to school but most of it would be stored. I left and found myself a cute little apartment close to campus.

Jake transferred his horse savvy to Windhaven as Brandi concentrated her energies toward the nationals. I felt a twinge of jealousy knowing I could have gone on to the internationals if I had been more serious about competing. My mother had been right. It was the first time I had let Fritz down. He was better off with Brandi. I was sure they'd make the internationals before Fritz would retire.

I still had the money for school that dad had set aside before he died. That was no concern. At this moment, however, sitting in my new apartment, it was the least I wanted. I wanted to compete. Why had I not taken it more seriously? Just to spite mom?

I vaguely remembered the fun I had gotten out of helping Brandi get into the horse experience by trading barn work for lessons. I remembered watching her bloom with confidence as her equestrian skills improved. I remembered the gratitude of her parents who couldn't afford the lessons at that time.

I saw the many faces of the other girls I had put astride the creatures that gave them joy.

Then, I realized, yet again, how fortunate I was to have grown up around the best teachers, trainers and horses Dad could afford. I could honestly say, looking from the outside of my life anyone would think I was born into the elite horsey set. Judging by Aunt Gwen's reaction, however, they still rejected me because of my pedigree. I guess I didn't have the mind set mom tried to drill into me that being the best was what counted.

Chapter 4

Bernadette Ellen Rhodebeck wasn't from money. She had working class parents that barely noticed their daughter, let alone what she was interested in. She was smart, however, and wanted to be more than working class. She managed to convince her parents that being valedictorian of her senior class warranted going to an elite college with horse related curriculum. The curricular activities weren't the initial draw. It was the elitism that gave the flame to her dreams of being more than her parents.

It was after she got there, and had put a semester under her belt, that she noticed the horsey set exuded the most money, gaiety, popularity; probably in that order. She had no doubt her parents couldn't afford a horse. It was all they could do to pay for the school. She'd have to infiltrate the world of horses some other way.

It was a wintry day in February that she wandered down to the barns. The smell was unusual but she was used to the stink of factory and noxious rivers so she wasn't repelled by it. She found an instructor who was just finishing up a lesson and stated her case. She was in business management but wanted very much to learn to ride. Was there any way she could get lessons on the side?

The schooling horses were for the equine curriculum only. She could, however minor in horse management which included stable office management, and animal insurances. She'd also have to pay the extra fee to use one of the school's horses. She could sneak in the extra courses without her parents raising a fuss, she was sure, but the extra fee for use of a horse was not feasible.

There was no prohibition for a student in the equine curriculum from giving lessons although not doing their own barn work during the week was considered cheating. So there were only the weekends to use as barter for lessons. There was no end to the equine students willing to let Bernadette clean their horses' stall and groom their mount on the weekend in exchange for riding lessons. So she gave up Saturdays and Sundays to clean stalls which entitled her to a riding lesson from each horse's owner.

Of course, they never accepted her into their social class. She was just a groom, after all. But she discovered she truly loved riding. She also discovered a whole class of equestrians struggling financially to hold onto their mounts and studies. She didn't fully assimilate in to the more humble group either, because it wasn't her view of herself.

After two years of watching Bernadette's efforts, an instructor offered her more consistent lessons in exchange for taking over care responsibilities of her private mounts, a position vacated by a graduating senior. Bernadette even got to compete in a private show now and again. More often, however, she acted as groom for several students at school-sponsored horse shows.

It was at one such show that Daniel Kurt saw her putting finishing touches on several horses waiting for their riders. Her blond hair was pulled back into a pony tail but several strands had escaped. She had manure smudged on her pants and horse slobber on the sleeve of her sweat shirt.

"Boy, you are filthy," he said by way of greeting. An unlit pipe was clenched between his even white teeth. His hands were in the pockets of his pants. His hair was parted on the side and combed back.

Her blue eyes swung his way, looked him up and down and swung back to the horse she was working on. She said nothing. He waited awhile and then walked away.

She had twelve to fifteen minutes between riders mounting up and getting the next horse spiffed up for competition. No time to think of a young man with a pipe between his lips. But after the last competitor took their horse and entered the practice ring, her job done, she went to the side line to watch the remaining classes. There were still several to be completed. The young man appeared at her side again. He said nothing at first, watched the horse incur a fault before he spoke up.

"Do you really enjoy playing in the muck?"

She didn't even look at him when she answered. "I prefer to ride but playing in the muck is part of the game."

"Not if you get someone to do it for you."

"Yes, well, it gets me a bit of riding for myself and sometimes some pocket money."

"You don't spend it on your horse?"

"I don't have a horse."

"I'm Daniel Kurt, by the way." He held out his hand.

"Are you sure you want to shake my filthy hand?"

"Did you wash them?"

She looked at him. "No."

"Oh, well..." He stuck his hand back in his pocket. "I'm sure you still have a name."

"Bernadette Rhodebeck."

"Do your friends call you Berny?"

"No. They call me Bernadette."

"I see."

The horse in the arena balked at the obstacle. The rider came off and slammed into a side pole, knocking the whole jump apart. "Ouch," Bernadette sympathized along with the rest of the audience as she watched the rider pick herself up and limp after the horse. A crew of arena attendants quickly reassembled the pieces.

"You seem too smart to think that would be fun."

"And how would you know how smart I am?"

"You have to be smart to go to this school."

"How do you know?"

"My sister is Gwen Kurt. She's number one fifty nine. I pointed you out and she said you're a junior and a half." He chuckled.

She smiled at that. Taking classes during the summer months had gotten her a semester ahead.

"She actually has smile muscles," he said as he gazed at her. He must have seen a look of shock on her face because he added, "You always look so intense. You should smile more."

"I'll keep it in mind."

Bernadette Rhodebeck didn't marry money, although he came from money. Daniel Kurt loved her. Their house was just a ranch but he kept the stalls full for her. Gustavo was probably the only recipient of her love. All the horses before him were only for her aggrandizement and Daniel was to supply the means to the aggrandizement.

To her credit, she was aware of how much "horse" her husband could afford and still hire the necessary trainers and instructors. She took those horses to their peak ability. To me, that was more of a success than Carley Carlyle wasting her national champion dressage mount, Sassy Murdock, by not entering higher classes, not challenging her to improve because she was afraid of taking home less than a first place.

Dad was an English/History major doing graduate work when he introduced himself to mom. He went straight to university teaching. I suppose that's where I got my love of teaching, even if it was just teaching riding and horse care.

The main reason I competed was to give credence to our equestrian center. I loved to ride but I didn't really care if I won or not. I only cared about whether my horse and I worked as a team and if we improved. It got us our share of ribbons even though a lot of shows were just stepping stones in our advancement, much to mother's chagrin. What I really enjoyed was to share the joy of riding with others. If they wanted to compete, fine. I was capable of taking them to that level. If not, that was fine, also.

Mom on the other hand was a true blue competitor and what I had viewed as a storybook life, she had viewed as far short of her dreams. I was a wrench in the cogs of her plans. She sold her last eventing horse and bought Gustavo. Without the pressure of trying to earn acceptance, she was free to love for the first time, and Gustavo was there to receive it.

Maybe she finally understood she would never be accepted into the inner core of the elite horse set because of her pedigree, not her competition status. Perhaps she didn't realize she had their respect. Or maybe that wasn't enough. She wanted to be 'them'. For whatever reasons, she made me feel it was my fault she gave up the effort, and transferred the mantel of her dream to my shoulders.

I, of course, didn't want to carry it.

Dad told me to pursue what would make me happy and the rest would take care of itself. Despite his dislike of the barn, he was always there for my shows. His observation skills always noted improvement even if no ribbon came home. I suppose his praise enabled me to handle mom's caustic critiques instead of crumbling beneath them.

By the time I was twelve, the Kurt's Equestrian Center had three horses I had outgrown, on which to give lessons. It also took in boarders. It was bringing in money that was put into my equestrian career and took the financial load off Dad while I planned to be anything but a competitor.

Chapter 5

I stumbled into my small apartment, locked the door, dropped the mail on the coffee table where it buried the last two un-opened letters from Jake. I started disrobing as I made my way to the bed. I crawled, naked, under the sheet and fell asleep instantly.

A late morning sun caressed my face into wakefulness. My eyes opened slowly as did my brain. How many days had I slept? I had felt like I could sleep for a month after I had completed the last exam of the semester and stumbled back to my apartment with exhaustion grabbing at my ankles.

I wasn't sure I wanted to get up yet. I lay there debating, waiting to see if I would sink back into oblivion. I heard the phone ring in the living room. I let the machine take it.

"Madison, where the heck are you? Are you alright? Dr. Goodson is wanting to talk to you about a position. He can't hold it forever! Call, call, call."

I opened my eyes to a sun-filled room. My plants seemed to stretch as they soaked up the vitamin D. I groaned. Would

I ever think in normal terms again or forevermore in medical relations?

I sat up. I didn't sway. That was encouraging. I stood and walked toward the bathroom. No stumbling so I must be rested. I took a hot shower and felt much better. I donned a short terry robe, opened the French doors to the balcony, stretched to a breeze and late spring bird song. It was good to see green again.

The leaves were full so I'm sure the green had been around for awhile. I'd just been too busy to notice. It had been non-stop since starting vet school, using breaks and summers to work in the required various internships at research centers, animal hospitals, and private practices to get experience and a feel for which direction I wanted to plot my life.

I had trudged through dusty heat, grey rain, white snow storms, brown mud, green shadows and then repeated the cycle again for four years. At last it was over. I was determined to take a couple weeks off to reconnect with the other world out there.

I had already made some decisions. Research was definitely out. I knew it was important work but I couldn't do it. I was leaning heavily toward Equine medical centers but was still also considering a large/small animal practice.

In the refrigerator was a cardboard carton of orange juice. I opened its lips and took a whiff. It still smelled okay. I poured a tall tumbler full. There were three eggs left and a piece of whole wheat bread without any green on it. The eggs were soon sizzling and the bread was in the toaster. As the aroma wafted around me, I realized I was famished.

I was going to have to go shopping for groceries for sure. For now, however, I chewed my breakfast, savoring the experience of eating slowly, allowing each flavor to move around my mouth, dancing with my taste buds and finally, almost in liquid form, slide down my throat. When the plate was empty, I rinsed it and put it in the sink, took the half full tumbler of

OJ and went to the living room. I finally found the answering machine under pages of a research paper's rough draft. I hit rewind and then play.

"Madison? This is Julie. Dr. Goodson is requesting you as his assistant. Call and say yes."

"Madison, this is me again. Did you get my last message? Call Dr. Goodson and say yes."

"Madison, Dr. Goodson is getting impatient. The correct answer is yes.

"Madison, this is Jake, did you get my letters? We're next door in Preoria for a big show on June 17th. Come watch Brandi and Fritz wipe out the competition."

"Madison, this is Daryl. We gotta party at least one night before we become adults with our noses back to the grindstone. Call me."

"Madison, where the heck are you…"

I hit the delete button, dialed Dr. Goodson's office and told his receptionist, "No".

Then I dialed Julie. "What's the date?"

"The tenth. Where've you been?"

"Sleeping. I thought I'd been asleep for days but I guess it's only been about sixteen hours."

"Well, you probably needed it. I've been trying to get hold of you for three days. Did you call Dr. Goodson?"

"Yes. I said no."

"Madison! You passed on that opportunity?"

"Afraid so. I really don't want research."

"But the teaching opportunity afterward."

"I just can't do it."

"Then what?

"Take some down time."

"You won't know what to do with down time."

"All the more reason to take some and learn how to handle it again."

"Where are you gonna start?"

I chuckled. "Around here. I'll return a couple phone calls, open mail I haven't looked at for weeks, go get groceries, go shopping." I was already moving, sorting sheets of paper and envelopes into "keep" and "pitch" piles. The rough draft was old news and was followed by the junk mail into the "pitch" pile. There were envelopes from places I had sent some resumes as well as two letters from Jake and one from Brandi.

"Well, if you're serious about taking it easy for awhile, give me a call if you want to go do something. When do you take your boards?"

"July tenth. Let's go to the pool on Thursday to soak up some sun if it's nice."

"It's supposed to be hot for the next several days, so I'll see you there. About tenish?"

"That'll work. See you then."

I hauled the "pitch" pile to the trash can and then opened both of Jake's letters. The first was dated just after Christmas.

"Dear Madison,
Sorry you couldn't make it home for Christmas AGAIN. Sounds like you're pushing yourself pretty hard. Don't forget to take time to smell the roses...or horses.

There's a National show in Preoria that Brandi and Fritz will be competing in on June 17. Mark it on your calendar. I'll even come pick you up. Surely if we're that close, you can't miss it.

My insurance business is really taking off. I really like being my own boss. I can put in lots of hours and then ease off when I want to do something like watch Brandi compete.

And what a competitor she is. I can honestly say she and Fritz have been good for each other.

Take care. Hope to see you in June.
Jake

Enclosed was a picture of a very fit Fritz posing for the camera. My heart constricted with jealousy. It still hurt to have let him go and for someone else to have taken him to his peak. I had to admit Brandi did him justice and I probably wouldn't have gone as far with him. I knew Jake thought he was being nice sending pictures and articles of their climb through the show ranks. Mom would have been proud of her, I thought. They just didn't realize what a small person I was and how it rankled.

The next letter was dated May 15th.

Dear Madison,

I had hoped to get a letter from you saying you could make the show in Preoria on June 17th. Brandi and I would both love to have you there.

I know your last letter said you were working hard on your studies and internships. Your penmanship showed you need some downtime. Don't have a nervous breakdown.

Please let me pick you up for the show. It's on June 17th. My number (in case you've forgotten) is 780-438-5151.

Take care of yourself,
Jake

Enclosed was a picture of Brandi and Fritz sailing over a five foot fence.

I dialed Jake's number.

"Andrew's insurance agency," answered a feminine voice.

"May I speak to Jake please?"

"May I ask who's calling?"

"Madison Kurt."

There was a pause and then Jake's effusive voice seemed to scintillate into my ear, down the Eustachian tube, tickled my throat and settled on my heart. I felt such a feeling of nostalgia I almost cried and didn't know why.

"Madison, it's great to hear your voice. Can you make the show?"

"You bet. Still want to pick me up?"

"Absolutely. Oh six hundred okay? We'll get breakfast on the way."

"Sounds good. See you then."

I gave Jake directions to my apartment and then opened Brandi's letter.

Dear Madison,

Are we torturing you with the pictures and articles of Fritz and me? If so, I do apologize but I hope all you feel is pride in giving us both a chance to make it big in eventing. I thank you from the bottom of my heart. Fritz thanks you too. You made US possible.

I hope you'll be able to come to the show on June 17th. We'll be so close, it would be a shame to not take advantage of it. Still, I don't want to open an old wound, so if you can't come, I'll understand.

Love,
Brandi

What a perceptive young woman Brandi was. She knew what a small person I was and still wanted me to be there. Well, I'd just have to work on shutting out the jealousy and being happy that Brandi rescued Fritz before I had totally wasted his potential.

My eyes were starting to burn. I knew I could go back to sleep but I forced myself to call Daryl and arrange for a night out, then vacuumed and changed the bed sheets between which I then crawled and went back to sleep.

Over the next couple days I alternated between activity and sleep although the naps were becoming shorter. I watched some rented movies, stocked my refrigerator, went out for Chinese and karaoke with Daryl, caught up on laundry and was working on spring cleaning the apartment. I had even walked to the park to sit beneath a tree. I watched people and animals from my blanket; listened to the leaves rustle overhead and fell asleep with the breeze running its fingers over my face.

By the evening of June sixteenth, I was feeling almost human again. I got a full nights sleep and was up and waiting when Jake knocked at my door. I'm sure I had a smile on my face when I opened the door but Jake's face registered shock. He quickly flashed a smile and said, "Hungry?"

"Famished."

"There's a little place half way between here and Preoria. Can you make it to there?"

"I'm sure. Let's go."

"So how long have you been a free woman?"

I laughed. "Since the tenth."

He kept glancing at me. "How does it feel?"

"Great. What's wrong?"

"Nothing, why?"

"Why do you keep looking at me funny?"

"Well, number one, I've missed you. Number two, gosh Madison, have you looked at yourself lately? You're a skeleton. Your clothes are just hanging on you. Don't you eat?"

I laughed. "I guess I do when I have time. Don't worry. I'm sure I'll gain a hundred pounds now that I'm out of school."

"You could probably stand to gain that much. What have you been doing with yourself?"

"Oh, catching up on all the movies I've missed over the last four years, read a book for enjoyment instead of research or to pass a test, listening to the wind through the trees, working on my tan poolside."

"Sounds great. How did you do in school?"

"Upper five per cent of my class. Unless I totally blow the boards, I'll soon be a bona fide veterinarian."

"So all that hard work paid off."

"Yep."

"Know where you're going yet?"

"I've interviewed at the Animal Medical Center at Columbus, Ohio. I have an interview at another Medical Center in Musky, Connecticut next week. I've interviewed at several small and large animal clinics around the state."

"Anywhere close to home?"

"Montaine is the closest, I think."

"That's about forty miles west of us, isn't it?"

"Something like that. It's a small animal clinic. Dr. Flowers is planning to retire in about two years."

We pulled into Purdy's Diner and ordered our breakfast.

Jake continued. "You don't have any desire to settle closer to home?"

I hesitated. "It doesn't feel like home, Jake. It's not like I have a proud family to welcome me home, you know. They were pretty clear that the Center was no longer my home."

"What about opening your own place?"

"Gee, I haven't thought of that since starting vet school. There just hasn't been time to think of anything but studying the past four years. I chose a course, and that's pretty much been my focus."

Our waffles, bacon, orange juice and coffee arrived. We busied ourselves with eating.

When Jake pulled the truck next to the blue and silver horse trailer at the show grounds, the first person I saw was Shelly sitting on a bale of yellow straw. I made a mental note that she had lost weight. I was glad to see she had moved up to professional groom. Brandi was grooming Fritz as he lazily munched on a few wisps of hay. I was glad to see she still participated in his care to keep a close personal connection with him. The pictures I had received hadn't done him justice. His coat gleamed over firm muscles. There wasn't an ounce of fat on him.

Brandi looked up with a smile for Jake. Her eyes slid to me and although the smile remained, for a split second there was question in her eyes which she couldn't keep out of her voice. "Madison?" She threw her arms around me and gave me a hug, the brush grazing my ear.

"Yeah, it's me. Hi Shelly," I said over Brandi's shoulder. She waved with leg wraps in her hand.

Fritz threw up his head at the sound of my voice. "Hey there fella." He whickered and pulled at his lead. "You remember me?" I felt a thrill run through me as we put our heads together as we used to. His horsey aroma touched with the smell of polishes and fly repellent prickled my skin. The fragrances of leather and hay wafted together and created a longing in me I'd not felt for years.

"Maybe you two need some time alone."

I heard the words and was grateful they didn't stay to watch the tears squeeze out from under my closed eyelids. Fritz seemed to be content to stand there head to head as well. After awhile I picked up a soft brush and stroked his sleek brown body and ran my fingers through his black mane and tail. His head dropped back to finish his hay.

A short while later, Jake, Brandi and another gentleman returned.

"Madison, this is my fiancé, Russell Lang."

I reached out my hand to shake his. "Hello, Russ."

"Madison, I've heard a lot about you."

"Russ opened his practice two years ago close to our area. His clientele is really picking up. He could use a partner." Brandi grinned and added, "Hint, hint."

"I'd be honored to consider your resume, Madison."

"I wouldn't want to cause trouble between you love birds if you should find it necessary to reject me."

"I think our relationship could handle that."

"He wouldn't dare, reject you. You're hired." Although she had a grin on her face, defiance was in Brandi's eyes and voice.

Shock crossed Russ' face. Jake and I laughed.

The announcer could be heard in the arena. "I'd better get ready," said Brandi. As she disappeared into the RV, Shelly emerged to start braiding Fritz's mane.

"Let's go get our seats, Madison." Jake took me by the elbow and guided me toward the stands. "Will you consider submitting your resume to Russ?"

"I'd rather not put him under pressure to hire me if he doesn't want me."

"I don't think he'd have a reason not to hire you."

"Well, he was a bit shocked at Brandi's insistence. He'd be hard pressed to be objective."

I heard hoof beats in the arena. My blood raced. My legs itched to be laying against a surging equine body. I caught my breath as the horse in the arena took the oxer and suddenly I couldn't care less where I worked. I just wanted on a horse. Wherever I chose to settle, I knew my first act would be to find a horse to get on, even if it was a leased mount.

Chapter 6

Russell Lang's growing small and large animal practice was in Dockside, thirty miles toward Groveport. I had gotten word last night from Jake that he had hired a new grad by the name of Daryl Stadler. I had to grin at the news.

Dr. Flowers' small animal clinic was the only animal care facility in Montaine. I settled just inside Montaine because I liked the community, I loved Dr. Flowers, I wasn't ready to limit myself to a one species practice and frankly, I was feeling good about being close to people I knew. Jake was fairly close; Daryl was even closer.

Montaine had a lot of trees; a park for people complete with a swimming pool, and even a dog park complete with swimming hole and agility course. The stores were small mom-pop establishments. Everyone was friendly. Probably hoping to learn everybody else's business but still it was nice.

Dr. Flowers had never married, had adopted four dogs and two cats over the years. He lived simply and put most of his money back into the practice. His surgical suites were top of the line. I was impressed and pleased. He lived above his clinic. I found out he even had a stand stall out back and did some equine first aid and preventative care if they trailered the horse to the clinic.

I had a small apartment near the park and utilized the pool quite often deepening my tan. The apartment was cramped and had small windows. The pastel colors lightening the walls did little to make it feel or look any bigger. I left most of my stuff in storage as I was actively looking to buy a house. In my left over time that is, and there wasn't much of that. The office hours were great. We alternated "call" for emergencies.

Once in awhile Daryl called. Leave it to him to find a karaoke place a bit north in Drummond. Jake came when he could to share sun and water. He called in between pool dates just to chat. Sometimes it was about being ready to get a horse of his own. With Russ on Brandi's arm, it was time for Uncle Jake to bow out and get a life of his own. He didn't want to board at Kurt's Equestrian Center but Windhaven had a waiting list. He wasn't sure what to do. It was time to open my Equestrian stables, he kept hinting.

His talk reminded me I had planned to put horses back into my life. I ran an advertisement asking for a horse to lease. I had two calls within a week. I drove out to the McMullen place the next evening. They were an elderly couple. The horse had been their granddaughter's but she was off to college and her parents wanted to send him to the auction. The McMullens wanted a better solution but were having trouble with the expenses and hadn't been able to sell him.

Spiffy Zip came when called, was a fifteen year old Quarter Horse gelding. His home was five acres of well maintained pasture with only a three sided wind break for shelter but it was cleared of manure. The water trough was clean and he was well groomed except for his hooves which needed trimmed. He was a bit overweight. Lack of grain in his diet hadn't hurt him any. He was friendly but according to the McMullens, he hadn't been ridden on the trails for three or four years. Since arriving on their farm seven years ago, he had never been asked to load in a trailer.

A western saddle sat on a homemade saddle rack. It was a milk can on metal legs with wheels. Mr. McMullen said it was kept inside the house and he polished the saddle sometimes just to occupy his hands in the evenings. As we tacked up Zip, Mr. McMullen explained that he really enjoyed caring for the horse. It was just the expense that was getting difficult to handle.

Spiffy Zip looked a bit surprised that he'd have to work after all these years but he stood placidly waiting to see what would happen next.

"I don't want to ride until those hooves are trimmed. Do you mind if I listen to his heart and lungs?"

"Go right ahead," they both urged.

I listened to heart, lungs and bowel sounds. They all sounded fine. His eyes were clear and there was no nasal discharge. I wanted to check him for soundness but an idle horse could go lame from just a little unaccustomed work, and again, those hooves needed tending first. I ran my hands over his legs and down his spine. I felt no hot spots.

"Did you want a contract signed? I don't think I can say at this point."

I could see the disappointment on their faces. "Let's get a Ferrier out here."

"But we..."

"I'll pay for it as well as his shots and wormer which I can administer now. We'll go from there."

"That's fine," they said, but I could see the worry on their faces.

As I got the necessary vaccines and an ivermectin wormer from the truck I assured them. "Even if I don't lease him, you'll be able to advertise him as current on shots and wormed. That might get some interested people to call."

Mr. McMullen had removed the saddle and bridle and held Zip by the halter. I punched the horse's neck with my fist to distract him and slid the needle in.

"I'm giving him a dose of bute as this one shot can cause some soreness." I gave another shot in his hip. Zip never flinched. He even took the wormer squirting in the side of his mouth fine but I knew horses didn't find the taste pleasant. The next time may not be as easy.

I would have stayed to groom him a bit but although the tools had been kept in the mud room of the house, they were worn down.

"I'll be back tomorrow evening if the day at the clinic isn't too bad."

I gave them a check made out to Curtis Rusneck, and his phone number. They assured me they would call him right away. Then they invited me back for dinner. I had intended to go see the other horse. It would be quite a drive there and back but I decided you can't have too many friends. I told them I'd love to.

I took a round about way to the other farm that raised Black Angus cattle, admiring the countryside, always looking for a suitable spot to call my own. I'd barely put the truck into park before a tall, lanky, dark-haired girl was beside it.

"Did you come to see Cherry Tart?"

"Is that the horse for lease?"

"Yes."

"Then that's who I'm here to see. Why is she for lease?"

"She's mine, but I can't handle her anymore. I used to be able to. She doesn't like me riding her anymore." The tears in the girls dark eyes made them glisten.

"Have you had a vet check her?" We were walking toward a three stall stable with paddock.

"Dr. Lang came and..."

"Arielle!"

We both looked toward the scowling woman and I realized they wanted someone to get the horse under control. They were hoping a new rider could fix the problem.

"You'll have to excuse my daughter. She's such a jabber box even if she doesn't know what she's talking about. The horse is just too much for Arielle but she throws a fit if we try to sell. So we thought we'd lease Cherry and get Arielle another."

"She's thrown…"

"Arielle!"

The girl's lips became a tight line across her face and a deep furrow formed between her eyes.

"Well, get her tack. Let's see if she's too much horse for me as well."

Arielle brought the tall Thoroughbred mare out of her stall and cross tied her. The horse stood calmly watching the people moving around her. I could tell Arielle had spent time grooming her before I got there. The red bay's coat gleamed like cherries in rain. No wonder she was named Cherry Tart.

While the tall teen in paddock boots, jeans, and a t-shirt that said Barn Goddess carried out an English saddle and bridle that looked new, I stood deep breathing the aroma of hay and horse. I felt my muscles relax. I wanted to close my eyes and float in the strong earthy smells.

"Wow, that's a gorgeous set. It doesn't look like it's been used."

"I've only had it a couple months and I like polishing it."

"How long have you had Cherry?"

"Four years. Of course, the first year as a three year old, she was at the trainers and I was taking lessons at Windhaven over in Groveport."

"So she's seven years old. Where's your old saddle?"

"I didn't have one. I rode bare back."

The mother broke in. "We bought the horse and paid for training and riding lessons. I thought she could at least pay for her own riding gear. It took awhile for her to save the money."

"I can understand that. Arielle, put the bridle on but not the saddle."

The mare gave her head to the bridle like a real lady. Arielle gave her some neck pats and an effusive "good girl".

"Does that surprise you?" I asked.

"She usually dances around and won't drop her head to put the bridle on."

"Do you usually put the saddle on first?"

"Yes."

"Did the problem start when you started using the saddle?"

Arielle's eyes widened. "Yes, I think so."

"Take her out to the paddock and I'll give you a leg up."

"I really don't want her on that horse."

I looked at the mother. I was a bit miffed that they'd endanger a stranger with a horse they expected to throw a rider but I could understand the desire to protect her daughter.

"I think it will be okay."

I could tell Arielle was a bit nervous also, but she gathered up the reins and bent her leg which I took hold of and lifted her onto the mare's bare back. "Go ahead and put her through some maneuvers."

The girl's cues were so subtle you could barely see them. They would be a knock out in a dressage ring, I thought. A smile split Arielle's face from ear to ear as she brought Cherry close to me, stopped and stroked the horse's neck. I patted the mare's red shoulder.

"I think your saddle is causing her pain. It's probably too small. You've taken good care of it. See if you can exchange it. Once you get a comfortable fit, I doubt you'll have any more problems or need anyone to lease her.

"Oh, thank you, thank you." Arielle leaned down from the horse and hugged my neck. "How can I ever thank you?"

"I'll think of a way. Give me your name and number so I can call you when I do."

"Arielle Adkins; 780-489-6000," she called as she opened the paddock gate from the back of Cherry Tart and cantered down the lane.

"I'll be calling you Arielle Adkins," I shouted after the retreating pair. I turned to the mother. "Mrs. Adkins, I'm Dr. Madison Kurt, Dr. Flowers' new partner at the Montaine animal clinic."

"Oh, yes." She held out her hand to shake mine but kept glancing at Arielle who was galloping on her friend across a field.

The sound of hoof beats echoed to my core. I longed to be astride a horse and galloping next to Arielle and Cherry Tart. Today had not gone as planned. I still didn't have myself a horse.

On that drive back to the McMullen's for dinner, I thought about Spiffy Zip. What was I doing? I wanted a horse to ride, not to rescue. Hopefully someone else would answer the ad with a horse ready to ride.

Chapter 7

The first person through the clinic doors the next morning was a waif of a child; blond hair, large blue eyes. She looked about four years old. She carried a huge cat draped over thin arms. It's tongue lolled out the side of its mouth. Dried blood and dirt stiffened its hair which smudged the child's pale arms and face.

I was just coming from the back to speak with Jennifer, our receptionist, who stood there with a look of horror on her face. I stepped back around the corner, slipped on a pair of latex gloves and grabbed a towel as I went through the door that led to the waiting room.

"Can I have the kitty, sweety?"

"Hurt."

"Here, let me wrap it in the towel, okay?"

"Hurt."

My gloved hand rested against the cat for a moment before I tried to wrap the towel around the cat but the little girl twisted sideways with her burden.

"Hurt."

"She's autistic," said Dr. Flowers coming from the back.

I hesitated not knowing how that translated into getting a dead cat out of her arms.

"Try holding the towel out and see if she'll put the cat to bed."

I held the towel in my hands. "Want to put the kitty on the bed so we can check it?"

"Hurt."

She started to walk around the counter towards the back. Dr. Flowers said, "It's alright. Let her bring it back herself. Jennifer, please call Gloria Ley. Tell her Cindy is down here."

Dr. Flowers stepped on a pedal that lowered a stainless steel examining table with a slow sigh. Cindy laid the cat on the shiny metal without any urging.

"I felt no warmth when I touched it," I said softly to Dr. Flowers.

"Hurt."

"He's very hurt, honey," I said.

She was reaching to push a strand of hair out of her eyes and I grabbed the dirty hand as gently as I could. Let's wash your arms, sweety."

"No. Hurt."

Dr. Flowers got a wet paper towel as I held the arm of the child that wouldn't move from the side of the cat.

"I don't see any breathing motion."

"The cat is hers," he said. "I usually let her listen to its heart."

I wiped the dirt and blood from her arms and face as he put his stethoscope in her ears. First he put the flat bell to her own chest until she smiled, and then onto the side of the cat. Cindy hesitated for awhile and then repeated, "Hurt."

Dr. Flowers took the ear pieces from her ears, put them in his own, and put the bell back to the side of the cat. I could see his mouth starting to form the word "dead" but he stopped as his eyes widened. "Madison, get a bag of LR's." He spun to a drawer to find an IV set and tourniquet.

As we scrambled, I heard Cindy say, "Hurt," and Mrs. Ley calling hysterically from the waiting room, "Cindy, Cindy, where are you?"

I almost didn't go out to see Spiffy Zip that evening. The whole day at the clinic seemed to match the pace set by Cindy, her cat and hysterical mother. Mrs. Ley wanted everything possible done for Cindy's cat. X-rays showed a head trauma and a broken right front leg. The cat was stable and resting.

Dr. Flowers and I were both a bit chagrined that we had assumed the cat was dead. The lolling tongue, the amount of blood, lack of breathing motions and body warmth had us assuming the worst.

Mrs. Ley was even more embarrassed. Cindy had gone to their room at three A.M. saying "Molly – hurt."

They assured her that Molly was out hunting mice. They were horrified to find Cindy gone when they got up at seven. They and several neighbors were searching the surrounding area for their daughter, who was actually six despite her diminutive size, when they were called by Jennifer at the clinic. No one knew how far Cindy had to go to help her cat and then carry it to the doctor.

As I drove out to the McMullen place, I wondered how Cindy had known her Molly was hurt. Were autistic children on a wave length closer to animals?

I was delighted to see Zip's hooves had been trimmed. Phil McMullen said as soon as Curtis heard it was for me, he said he'd be out at six thirty the next morning to get it done before his other appointments. I made a mental note to invite Curtis and his wife out to dinner.

I had picked up a set of grooming tools the night before. I set to work picking each hoof, brushing his coat, squirting detangler on Zip's mane and tail to help my fingers slide through the long coarse strands. I could tell he'd already been groomed that day. Phil definitely took good care of him.

It was all I could do to stay off of Zip for the first few days. I wanted to just spend time grooming and getting to know him before I asked him to accept me as a rider. Then I put him on a lunge line for a few more days to get his joints and muscles working again. He was unsure of my stretching his legs and neck but he liked the carrots that encouraged his efforts.

Finally I tacked up and swung into the saddle. Phil assured me that once upon a time, Zip had been road safe. We headed down the lane. I needed to know what he could or couldn't do. I tried shifting my weight and giving leg cues. Zip ignored them all. I squeezed my fist around the reins, pulled gently, then harder, until he stopped. It took a good hard kick in the ribs to get him going again and I was sorely disappointed that I literally had to pull his head around to get him to turn.

I had a flash back to a thought I had once had that any back yard horse would have made me happy. I realized now, that wasn't so.

We were headed back toward home. He made no effort to run so at least he wasn't barn sour. I let my pelvis sway gently with his long smooth stride and thought maybe he'd make a great egg and spoon contest horse. A far cry from what I wanted. And then I heard it; the clip, clop, clip, clop of his steady hoof beats and a smile stretched across my face.

There was a message from Jake on my machine when I got home from my first ride on Zip. "Madison, isn't this your weekend off?" How about spending the day house hunting. I've got a couple leads for you in your area. Then we'll top the day off with dinner. Let me know."

I called his number and got his home machine. "Are you a realtor now, also?" I chuckled. "Come by early; eightish and I'll make you breakfast. See you then."

Chapter 8

Jake and I stood looking at the buildings as rain slid down our slickers and hit our boots with hollow thuds. It dribbled from our hoods onto our faces. The wind blew it against our jeans. The wet was cold against our skin; a sure sign Fall was not far off.

I kept pivoting to take in the scene before me. The old farm house, a bank barn, an empty T-shaped horse stable, an indoor arena, and pastures. Beyond them were the rolling fields until they reached the woods. I finally stopped and looked at Jake. He was grinning from ear to ear. I punched his arm. "You knew I'd love this place! Why did you show it last? Why not skip the other two places and go straight to here?"

"For comparison purposes...and to spend more time with you." He laughed, grabbed my hand and pulled me toward the stables.

"This is the old Ballard Quarter Horse breeding facility," he said as he pushed the white door open along its track. "In fact, this is where your trusty mount Spiffy Zip was born. When old man Ballard died thirteen years ago, Mrs. Ballard, never a breeder at heart, rented it out to horse lovers over the years. She kept raising the rent until no one wanted it anymore. She's been ailing for several years and died last week. There are back taxes due and kids that are waiting for their inheritance."

We were walking down the aisles looking at moldy straw in the stalls. It smelled of accumulated dust. The stall walls and doors were still solid. The high ceilings provided good ventilation. The rough concrete between the rows of stalls was without cracks. The arena was large. The sand needed raked to break up the dirt clumps and collect the litter of leaves. Several spots were muddy where the rain had come through a few holes where the vinyl skylights were missing.

The rain had stopped and we trudged to the house. Jake had the key as the realtor, Marshal Provost, was a friend of his. We took off our muddy boots on the inside porch so we wouldn't leave a mess, and walked in stocking feet over the cold hardwood floors, up the stairs and through carpeted rooms. It might look like an old farmhouse on the outside but the inside was elegantly renovated. From the fireplace, to the huge windows revealing a small forest of evergreens surrounding the back yard, it called my name and I answered "Yes."

We went back to my place to get a shower. With a glint in his eye, Jake suggested we share it. I just laughed and told him to get on with his. He had brought a suit to change into which meant I needed something a bit nicer than the clean jeans I had planned on. Well, basic black would do with cubic zirconium high lights.

Two hours south of Montaine, on the outskirts of Damascus, in a ritzy, glimmering place called Diamonds, we ordered Boston Strip and Sirloin tips.

"So what are you going to name your place?"

"Phoenix Stables."

"Great name. It'll rise up from it's own dust piles."

"Exactly."

"Going to pay cash?"

"No; twenty percent. I'll need a lot to clean up the place, put up new fencing, repair the arena skylights. I'll need schooling horses. I'll get the house cleaned up first so I can get moved in."

"As soon as you're ready for a boarder let me know. My horse will be the first in the place."

"Jake, I didn't know you had finally got yourself a horse."

"I don't yet, but I can start looking now."

"What are you looking for? Maybe I can help you to repay the debt I owe you for finding the Ballard place for me."

"Oh, Quarter Horse type. Just something to ride."

"Jake, you can come ride the horses anytime you want. You don't have to invest in one of your own unless you really want. You know there will always be horses needing exercised at the stables."

"I might be there more than you want me."

"You're always welcome," I said as I took a bite and looked up at him. He had stopped chewing and was simply looking at me. I gasped and that bite of food rushed to the back of my throat to put me in a coughing frenzy.

"You okay?"

Napkin to my mouth and still coughing, I nodded.

"Russ and Brandi have finally set a date. Next April eighteenth."

I swallowed some water. "That's great. Will she continue to compete?"

"No. She's gone about as far as she thinks she can. They haven't done all that well internationally. There are a lot of great horses on the international circuit. She wants to finish her last year of college and then settle down into career, marriage and babies."

I nodded but was afraid to look up at him and was grateful when he looked down at his beeper which must have been on vibrate.

"Will you excuse me, Madison?"

"Sure."

My mind felt like a whirly gig. When had Jake shifted emotional gears? I thought we were friends. That look he had given me held more than friendship. I thought back over the last six or seven years that I had known him from the time he came to work as a stable hand at Kurt's Equestrian Center. He had always been nice, cheerful, a conscientious worker. He treated the horses with respect and was helpful with the students, instilling knowledge and confidence wherever needed.

Now that I thought about it, I'd never seen him with a girl. But then I only saw him at the stables. He was a fantastic friend. He kept sending encouraging letters and leaving phone messages that often brought a smile to my tired face as I plowed through college and vet school. He never fawned over me, or pushed himself on me. I had assumed there were other recipients for that area of his life.

My mind then took a side track. How in the world had I made it to the twenty-sixth year of my life without having one sexual affair? I stared at the remains of my sirloin tips and wondered if something was wrong with me.

Jake returned to the table. "Sorry. That was a client. He and his wife have been in a serious accident. They're both in the hospital. She's unconscious. I told him to get some rest and I'll be there in the morning to see him. Normally, I'd go right away but I'm already busy with something important at the moment."

I looked up at him. "What career is Brandi considering?"

"Actually, she wants to go into insurance with me."

"How do you feel about that?"

"It would be great. I could expand over your way. Let her work the established clients in and around Groveport."

I swallowed.

"How do you feel about that?" he asked.

"I'm sure there's enough business to support you both."

He smiled a sad sort of smile and replied, "I see."

I felt a stab in my heart realizing I had just hurt a very good friend.

"Have I ever told you how much I enjoyed all the letters and phone messages you sent through those eight years I struggled through school?

"No, I don't think you have. I'm glad you enjoyed them."

"I'll bet they're what kept me going. You're the best friend anyone could ever have."

"Are you emphasizing 'friend'?"

"No, I'm trying to emphasize how much you mean to me and what a hole it would leave in my life if you weren't in it."

"Will you marry me?"

"I will."

The smile that took over Jake's face added to the feeling that those two words were the most natural reaction to his question. There was no doubt in my mind that Jake would be a great addition to my life and the best man with which to spend the rest of my life.

As we drove home we chatted about our plans for Phoenix Stables. He would call Marshall on Monday to start negotiations. All our chatter, however, couldn't drown out my mother's faint voice from the other side. "Marry money, Madison. I want you to be happy." I couldn't imagine being any happier than what I was at this moment.

At one point I caught Jake staring at me. "Eyes on the road, please, or we won't live long enough to get married."

He glanced back at the road. "I am going to give you the best ever wedding present."

"A trip to Hawaii?"

"Don't even try to guess because I won't even say cold, warm or hot."

We pulled in at my place. I asked hesitantly, "Are you coming in?"

He grinned. "Well, yeah. I need to get my wet clothes."

On his way back out he set his wad of wet things on the floor, took my face between his two hands and kissed me. "I love you. See you tomorrow."

He was gone and yet I stood there feeling like I was electrically charged. Gradually the sparks quit firing. With just two words, I had redirected my life. Could it be as simple as that?

I sat and thought over the past years. I'd had a suitor and hadn't even noticed. I'd been so wrapped up in horses and school, I'd just assumed Jake would always be there. I smiled as I thought that wasn't a good beginning. I was not even married and I had already taken him for granted. I vowed I would never do that again.

I was grateful, however, that I had established myself first. Maybe I wouldn't have succeeded had I thought I had a man to lean on. Once again it struck me how fortunate my life had been with the opportunities presenting themselves and having the means to take advantage of those opportunities. I felt a chill and shivered. Would fate someday demand a reckoning to balance the books?

I lit some aromatic candles, made a cup of herbal tea and sat down with The Magic of Horses, a new volume of true horse stories. But my brain wouldn't focus on the sentences so my eyes quit focusing on the words. I stared into space and saw Phoenix Stables materialize. I decided to accept boarders right away. As I found and purchased schooling horses, I'd establish the riding center. I smiled as I realized I could hardly wait for my first pro bono case.

Chapter 9

Is it my imagination? Everything seems so vivid. From the deep verdant grass thriving on the Fall rains to the vibrant, wet Autumnal leaves. From Cindy's blue eyes to Molly's direct green ones. It almost seemed Molly was trying to communicate with me and Cindy was watching to see if I was picking up the transmission. Then I realized that lately all the animals were looking at me intently.

Odors in the clinic were suddenly sharp; aromas of wet earth and fallen leaves were fecund; the smell of paint pungent on my stables and arena; the new furniture, drapes and fantastic cooking from Jake's own hands lured me into a domesticity I'd never noticed before. Was it my imagination or was the sun really brighter the morning after I realized I loved Jake and he left with only his wet clothes? There had been a classmate who was into positive thinking and metaphysics that once said that "magic was simply a change in consciousness." I was struggling with grasping the knowledge we were drowning in. She seemed to soak it up like a sponge and the animals she worked with in her internships gravitated to her. I remember being jealous.

"Quit fighting for it, Madison. You already know it. Study is just a reminder."

I was having too much trouble with what was already before me to try to grasp metaphysical principles as well. So I continued to grapple until I pinned my opponent and fully understood the material.

But this...this change in view. I'm not even sure what changed other than the discovery that Jake loved me and I realized I loved him, as well. I felt like I had quit struggling, although I don't know what I had been struggling with or against. The shadow was gone and in its place was awareness; of how Jake looked, smelled, interacted with others; of the animals I touched and how they looked at me and responded to my touch; of Dr. Flowers with his kindly smile, his masculine smell, the twinkle in his eyes, his insistence that I call him Clint. It was hard to imagine I had not noticed these things before. Even Spiffy Zip seemed to be trying harder to understand giving his head to move his hindquarters.

I was chopping lettuce, cucumber and carrots in my very own Phoenix house thinking these thoughts. My hands quit working as my eyes traveled to Jake on the deck outside the sliding glass doors, wearing the GRILL SARGEANT apron I got him. The soft glow of a warm October afternoon gave him an aura of gold. He brushed more of his own homemade Bar-B-Q sauce on the skinless hunks of fowl he was grilling, wiped his hands on a towel and came inside.

"When did you become such a chef?"

"I had to do something with my time while waiting for you to grow up."

I threw a crinkle cut carrot slice at him. He caught it and popped it into his mouth.

"You cut a mean crinkle cut carrot Mrs. Andrews."

He turned to the oven to check the cheesy potatoes. I walked to him and put my arms around his waist as he stood up straight.

"We aren't married yet Mr. Andrews."

"There's a surprise for you in my pocket."

I slowly slid my hand inside his pocket until it touched the metal ring at the very bottom.

"Go ahead. Get it."

I slipped my finger through it and crooked the knuckle enough to be able to draw in back out.

"Oh, Jake. It's gorgeous."

He pushed the marquis-shaped diamond the rest of the way on my finger.

"I'm not sure I can wait another year to get married," he groaned.

"Then we'll get married when you say."

"But you wanted a Fall wedding and you need time to plan."

"Winter can be pretty, too. Or Spring. It's not like I have a lot of family to invite. It's mostly your family and our friends. Or it can just be us."

"You'd pass on a big wedding?"

"Jake, having you is more important to me than when or how big. I have an idea! Let's invite them for a New Year's Eve party and just after midnight we'll get married."

"I like that idea. I am marrying one creative woman."

He wrapped his arms around me and drew me to him. As our bodies met, I whispered, "Your chicken is burning."

My days off now had an urgency. I needed to find a dress much sooner. I needed a caterer. I was sure there were other things I needed that I hadn't thought of yet. The preacher would be explained with the job of blessing Phoenix stables. At just after midnight Jake and I would excuse ourselves and return in gown and tux. I was getting excited. This would be better than a big wedding.

My afternoons after clinic hours were spent with Spiffy Zip. He was really making progress. I was thinking of purchasing him as a schooling mount. He was steadfast and would be great for beginners, large and small. Mr. McMullen was going to be lost if I took Zip away. I had to come up with a plan to keep horses on his place and keep him occupied caring for them at no expense to him. Then it hit me. Maybe I could use his place as a quarantine and time out area for new horses, or mounts needing a break or get well time. I stopped in to see Arielle and Cherry Tart. The new saddle was a good fit and Cherry responded happily to Arielle's subtle cues. They had entered a local show several weeks ago and had taken home a first in the novice dressage class.

I wanted to know why I hadn't seen them at any of the other nearby shows. Arielle's face fell when I asked her. "I have to pay for the entrance fees and clothes myself. It just takes so long to save up the money."

"They are pricey aren't they?"

"As soon as I'm old enough, I'll apply for work at Gloria's diner and Red Oak boarding kennel. Maybe one of them will hire me."

"Red Oak is a good ways out. How will you get there?"

"Dad said he'll get me one way to any job. I'll have to find a ride for the opposite way."

"Well, if it's okay with your parents, would you like to work at Phoenix?"

Her eyes lit up. "Oh could I?"

"It would be dirty work; scrubbing buckets, cleaning stalls, laundering coolers and blankets, polishing tack, grooming and exercising idle horses. Everything you do for Cherry times a hundred."

Her mouth dropped. "You're going to have a hundred horses?"

I laughed. "Probably not. I was exaggerating. It will be harder to keep working with Cherry. I'll insist you keep your grades up. Think you can do it?"

"Yes, yes, yes. How many days can I work there?"

I laughed again, pleased with her eagerness. "Let's start with weekends and see how you do. If the grades are maintained and Cherry is still getting quality time, we'll see."

Arielle was one happy girl when her parents okayed her work hours and promised to sign the permission form. That weekend Jake and I would be checking out some schooling horses he had found on the internet. Hopefully, we'd have horses for her to care for by the following weekend.

Curt Rusneck signed on as our facility ferrier and Mr. McMullen seemed to take on new life when I asked if he'd be our "down time" caretaker. I couldn't believe how well things were going. Shelly called that evening asking for a reference. As Brandi slowed down her show schedule, she needed to move on to something more secure.

"Would you care to be barn manager for Phoenix Stables?"

There was silence.

"I'd probably need you to do stable work as well, work the horses, and give some lessons until our stalls are full and we can afford to hire more help."

"I'm astonished with the offer, Madison. I would love to manage Phoenix."

"Great. When can you start?"

"First of the month okay?"

"Yep. Come out and check out the apartment above the garage. That can be part of the bargain if it suits you."

"It's sounding better all the time."

"Go to the uniform shop in Groveport. Delores is the owner. She has my specifications for our uniforms. She'll fix you up. I'll let her know you're coming."

I couldn't believe how well things were going. I felt like a mother hen gathering her chicks. Not that these people needed mothering, but they were all important to me. It was almost like a family. Even Brandi said she'd give lessons one day a week. I ran a quarter page colored ad for boarders in Montaine's newspaper and posted flyers in surrounding towns. We had three calls to return that evening. People were dropping by to see the facility. The bank barn was filling up with hay and straw. New water buckets and feeding pans graced the stalls now mucked and filled with clean straw. Sweet feed, beet pulp, senior feed and oats filled the feed bins. Leg wraps, ice wraps, vitamins, corn oil, wormers, fly sprays, salves and first aid kits filled the shelves and refrigerators. Brandi stayed the weekend while Jake and I traveled the surrounding countryside and into the next state checking out the schooling horses we had found on the internet. Out of the eight we went to inspect, we brought home only three. By the time we got home with our starting string, five boarders were already in their stalls. I was going to need someone full time until Shelly could take over. I called Mr. McMullen who agreed to take a temporary full time position.

Marshall Provost developed a web page for us and we advertised on it as well as in equine magazines for schooling mounts. Our stable was in a "T" shape. The trunk, made up of ten stall would be for our private and schooling horses. The top of the "T" made up of twenty stalls would be for boarders. A grooming area and two wash bays made up the area between the top of the "T" and the indoor arena.

As we unloaded our treasures and put them into their stalls, I inhaled deeply of the equine aroma. The Phoenix was rising and my heart with it as the sound of hoof beats filled my life once again.

Chapter 10

I placed the flat bell against Molly's ribs. The ear pieces were in Cindy's ears. She smiled up at me.

"All better?" I asked.

"Molly happy."

"I'll bet she is with a best buddy like you." I looked at her mother. "I'd say she has a clean bill of health, Mrs. Ley."

"Thanks to you and Dr. Flowers. I'm so glad you've joined this practice."

"Thank you but the thanks goes to Cindy for finding Molly so quickly and bringing her here."

"By the way, we pass your stables on the way to visit my sister. Cindy just loves the yellow and orange barns and gets very excited when she sees the horses in the fields. I'm having a hard time keeping her in her car seat as we pass. I was wondering if maybe we could stop in to pet a horse. I'll do anything that might bring Cindy out of herself more and that I can use as a bribe to get her to work harder on her speech." She grinned sheepishly.

Cindy's eyes sparkled, "Horsey?"

"Sounds like a plan. I've got just the H-O-R-S-E. I'm on call this weekend so it'll have to be an evening or not until next weekend."

"How about Friday night? That way, if she's hyper from the experience, I don't have to worry about her not getting enough sleep before school or church."

"Friday it is."

Dr. Flowers came from an exam room. "So how are the wedding plans coming along?"

"I've got my dress picked out. I still need a caterer."

"There's a woman in Damascus that does a great job. I've gone to several functions that she has catered. I swear I can tell it's her job by the stuffed crab and pecan tarts. If you're interested I have her card."

"Yes, I am."

He handed me the card and I glanced at it before shoving it into the hip pocket of my jeans. It claimed, "Melissa Johnson, Caterer Exemplar."

I called the caterer's number when I got home from the clinic and left a message on her machine. I then went out to work Zip and the schooling horses Argo, Deek, and George. Argo was a seventeen hand warmblood with personality plus. I had the feeling he was going to be my favorite. Deek was a sixteen hand Thoroughbred that had never raced. He had passed through many hands. At first I was suspicious of why, but it seemed it was just his bad luck. George was a fifteen, two Morgan/Thoroughbred cross with a bit of an attitude but his gaits were smooth. I was very pleased with my short string of mounts. Jake was working with George. I loved watching him. A nip or kick met with three seconds of "you're gonna die, horse" action and then all was soft, gentle handling once again. Already George was rethinking his aggressive behavior. He didn't like the loud, physical results when he bit or kicked, but he did enjoy the crooning voice and caressing hands when he behaved.

Friday finally arrived and I discovered I was excited about Cindy coming to the Phoenix. I had no doubt Spiffy Zip could handle any squeals of delight she might emit. There was something more, however. I wasn't sure what I expected but I was sure Cindy's connection to Molly was not limited to her cat. I was eager to see if she could connect with any of the horses as I had read autistics could.

The horses had been brought in from the pastures by the time the Ley's arrived. Some of the owners were tacking up to ride. Other horses were standing at their stall guards munching hay or dribbling grain as they chewed and watched the barn activity.

I walked out to the car to greet the Ley's. Jake had groomed and was tacking up Zip. If I expected uncontrolled squeals, I was proved wrong. I could see she was fighting to get out of her car seat and the car faster than her mother could keep up with her. "Hi, Cindy," I greeted.

Her hands were clasped over her chest, her eyes wide as half dollars, her mouth shaped in an "O" as she walked into the barn.

Gerry Miller was leading her Thoroughbred down the aisle toward the arena. She saw Cindy coming toward them. I saw the uncertainty cross her face and her pace slowed as she looked up at me in askance if I had turned the place into a day care.

I held up one finger in silent request for a moment to see what would happen. Cindy stopped and looked up in rapture at the big bay gelding. The horse stopped and put his muzzle next to the child's face and whuffled softly.

Cindy closed her eyes standing cheek to cheek with the horse for a few moments and then the horse raised his head and stepped around the waif of a child that barely reached his chest. Cindy opened her eyes and clapped her little hands saying "happy, happy, happy."

Gerry shrugged and shook her head in confusion.

"I think you have a happy horse," I explained.

"I'm glad to know that," she replied as she patted Big Bet on his muscular neck and continued on their way.

Cindy was already walking down the aisle stopping before each horse. Sometimes she clapped her hands and smiled, or got a look of sadness and reached up to stroke a soft velvety nose before moving on. I tried to make a mental note of those horses in hopes of determining the reason of their unhappiness.

Finally she approached Zip still standing in the cross ties. Cindy walked up to the nose Zip lowered to greet her. She wrapped her arms around the horse's jaw and laid her forehead on his. I felt a twinge of nostalgia remembering how Fritz and I had stood head to head on many occasions.

"Are you ready for a ride, Cindy?" asked Jake as he crouched down to her level.

She let go of Zip and nodded.

"May I help you on?"

Again she nodded and Jake hoisted her into the saddle. Her face almost split in half with a smile. Jake gave her some mane to hold onto but by the time we got into the arena she had let go, sat up straight and let her body sway with Zip's long strides.

Jake snapped the lunge line onto the cavesson and fed out the line. Mrs. Ley looked a little nervous and even I thought it was progressing too fast. Zip, however, maintained a steady walk and Cindy quietly flowed in his wake. A strange car pulled into the parking lot. Jake saw me look out the huge arena doors and said, "Go ahead. We're fine."

It always amazed me at how he was always aware of everything going on around him and the patience he had with kids and horses. He'd probably give Cindy at least an hour ride and not mind a bit standing in the center while they circled him. It wasn't a mindless standing. He was watching his charges, large and small, for signs of potential strengths and tiredness. Jake was always alert, watching, assessing, filing information.

I paused before leaving the arena as Gerry put Big Bet into a canter. I needn't have worried. Zip ignored the big bay and continued his long strided circular walk leaving slack in the lunge line. I smiled and went out to greet the family of four piling out of the mini van.

"Hello," greeted the woman. "I'm Marjorie Sawyer. These are my children, Lisa, Taylor, Lori and Todd."

The woman was full of nervous energy as were her children. She was already moving toward the barns. When she saw I wasn't following but had engaged the fidgeting children in conversation she returned and fidgeted with them.

"Lisa, do you like riding?"

"No, but mom says it's a socially necessary skill; A good way to meet eligible men."

"Are you from Virginia or Kentucky, Mrs. Sawyer?" I asked trying to make eye contact.

"Why yes, Virginia. How did you know?"

"Lucky guess." I turned back to the children all dressed in jodhpurs.

"Lori?"

Lori wasn't fidgeting. "I love horses and riding and showing."

She was almost breathless in her excitement.

"Ah, here is the horse lover of the family, I'll bet."

Her eyes sparkled as she nodded her head enthusiastically.

"Taylor?"

The boy looked about sixteen but he blushed and I wondered if he was younger. "It's okay," he mumbled looking down as he kicked a stone.

"And Todd; do you enjoy horses and riding?"

Todd's brow was creased between his eyes and his lips were pulled into a thin line. "I hate it."

Lisa giggled. "They hate you too. That's why you've been dumped so many times."

"If you hate it why do you do it?"

"I insist," interjected Marjorie. "I feel it's a skill all well bred people should have."

"Mrs. Sawyer, I'm really sorry but we're just getting up and running. I don't have enough schooling horses yet for all four children. We could get Lori started since she's the one that really enjoys it."

"There are plenty of horses here."

"They're privately owned and being boarded here. They aren't schooling horses."

"My children have ridden for several years. They aren't beginners. Surely you can borrow enough advanced horses for a group lesson."

"I haven't seen your children ride so I'm not even sure they should be on an advanced horse."

The woman looked at me as if I had antennae coming out of my head.

"Perhaps we should go elsewhere."

I saw Lori's face fall as I recommended, "You might try Kurt's Equestrian Center in Groveport or Windhaven in Dockside."

"Are you trying to get rid of me?"

"No, but if I can't meet your needs, that's no reason to deny Lori the joy of riding. Both stables are well established and have or had, last I heard, several good schooling horses at many levels."

There was a moment of silent shock before she asked, "How soon do you plan to have more horses?"

"As soon as we can find them. It is time consuming. If your children are such good riders, why don't you purchase your own mounts?"

Her defiant face fell. I saw the glimmer of tears at the corners of her eyes before she took a deep breath to pull herself back up. "That's a bit more costly than lessons."

"Yes, it is."

"Could you perhaps do two children one day and two another?"

I heard a touch of pleading in her voice. I wondered why they didn't just go to Kurt's. Jake came so often I forgot what a drive it was for him. I tried again.

"Why not provide lessons for Lori who actually wants them and let the other three that don't care for them drop them or at least wait until we have more schooling horses available?"

I saw the muscles in her jaw tense. "They will all continue their lessons."

"I see. Where do you live?"

"Northwest of here in Wellington."

"So it would be a hardship to bring the children on separate days?"

Her voice dropped. "I'm afraid so. I can't afford private lessons."

"Do you have time available to bring two children on two separate days? I'll only charge for one group lesson."

"I can manage that if the days are Tuesdays and Fridays."

"I think that can be arranged. I'll want the girls on one day and the boys on the other. And Mrs. Sawyer, you'll have to trust me in how I instruct your children. There will be no telling me how, what or where. Understood?"

She hesitated and then acquiesced.

"When can we start?" piped up Lori, jumping up and down.

"Tuesday is fine with me, but I'll need the boys to come on Tuesday and the girls on Friday because of the horses' lesson schedule."

"Mom?"

Mrs. Sawyer smiled at her daughter. "That will be fine."

Todd kicked a stone angrily. Taylor shuffled toward the van. Lisa sighed, "Oh gosh, for just a moment I thought we were saved."

I felt a heavy feeling in my chest. I felt bad for the kids being forced into lessons. I had been forced but was fortunate that I, at least, had liked horses and riding. Except for Lori, these kids didn't even want to be on a horse. I wondered what the mother's motive was, especially since the lessons seemed to be a financial hardship. Either I had to find a way to change her mind or help the kids make the most of their situation.

Later that evening I told Jake about the family of reluctant equestrians.

"Why didn't you just tell her you'd give lessons only to Lori or none of them?"

I paused, contemplating my motives. "I don't know."

Chapter 11

My life was definitely getting full. Gone were the evenings of relaxing with a cup of tea and a book. Now I fell into bed exhausted and got up with my eyes refusing to open. A steaming shower usually got them peeking into a new day, and a cup of tea on the way to the clinic finished the task to keep them open.

Thanksgiving was two weeks away. Shelly had hired a good crew and modeled it after mom's plan. We paid more but expected more from our stable hands. They had enthusiastically helped decorate the facility with corn and pumpkins. Someone was always bringing treats and made them available in the break room: pumpkin roll, cider, cookies.

Mrs. McMullen came to donate time and energy. She kept the break room clean and stocked. She planted flowers and even occasionally helped launder blankets and coolers. When I protested, she guffawed and claimed it gave her a new lease on life.

Mr. McMullen helped pick stalls, mow the yard, clean the cobwebs out of corners and groom Spiffy Zip whom he said he missed terribly. They had smiles on their faces, a cheery hello for everyone on the grounds and helping hands for anyone needing them. Jake and I decided if it gave their life meaning, they could keep coming and planned a generous Christmas bonus as a way to thank them.

A trail ride was in the planning for the weekend before Thanksgiving. Jake, Phil McMullen, Clint Flowers and Ryan, a stable hand, were working on a clearing in the woods, using stumps and hewn logs for benches, leaving five foot tall trunks for hitching rails, building up the brush pile for a bonfire. Fliers were sent to neighboring towns inviting other riders with properly inoculated horses to join us for a small fee. Our own boarders, stable hands, and students could participate for free.

I was still playing phone tag with Melissa Johnson, the caterer, and beginning to wonder if I might have to start calling a different one.

Cindy and Zip were developing a unique relationship. They preferred bareback and even bridleless. Leave it to Jake to perceive what was transpiring and give them the chance to show their stuff. Of course, they had almost developed a whole dance routine before Mrs. Ley or I accidentally discovered the secret. Was it mental telepathy or subtle movements of Cindy's waif-like form that signaled Zip what to do?

It was the music that drew us from our routines. I was watching Lori and Lisa groom the horses they'd be riding. Mrs. Ley was, as usual, chatting with Betty McMullen in the break room. What we saw astounded us. Zip and Cindy were practically dancing together to Jingle Bell Rock. Zip pranced, half passed in both directions; went right and left, right and left in a collected canter, perfectly changing leads, serpentining down the center of the arena. He trotted in cadence in one spot with Cindy giggling and clapping her hands above her head. When the music finally ended, Zip was a bit winded.

"It's a short lesson today Cindy," said Jake. "Zip's really tired. He worked hard for you."

Gloria Ley's mouth hadn't yet closed. "Let's go Cindy."

"No. I have to walk Zippy."

Her mouth dropped open again.

Cindy put her hand on Zip's wet shoulder and they started around the arena together. As other horses came into the arena, Zip moved to the inside of Cindy to protect her from cantering horses and flying sand.

〜

We had added only one more horse to our string of schooling horses. Roxy was a big Quarter horse mare; quiet and forgiving; a lot like Zip. In fact I used the pair of them to test new students and gage their level of skill with horses.

Lisa and Lori had proved adept at riding. Lori was an eager, enthusiastic student. I felt confident putting her on Argo. Lisa was a bit mechanical but would do fine on Deek. Since Cindy had first dibs on Zip on Fridays, the Sawyer boys had to come on Tuesdays. The first time they arrived, Todd had clenched fists and Taylor looked everywhere but at me. I showed them where the grooming tools were and what to do to start.

"We have to groom?" scoffed Todd.

"Yep. That's part of being a horseman. It helps develop a relationship with the horse."

The furrow between Todd's eyes deepened and his lips pulled into the familiar thin lines.

"The halters are hanging on the door pegs."

Taylor calmly entered Roxy's stall, capably put on her halter, snapped on a lead and took her to the grooming bay. He fumbled a bit using the unfamiliar brushes but was gently giving it his best.

Todd slid Zip's door open and stood quizzically looking at the halter he was holding upside down. Zip watched him a moment and then came toward Todd as if to help the boy figure out the straps, rings and buckles. Seeing the horse moving toward him, Todd dropped the halter, stepped back and slid the stall door shut with a bang.

"I'll bet it's hard to ride if you don't trust the horse isn't it?" I slid the door back open and bent to pick up the halter. "This part goes over the head and rests behind the ears. This circle here is the nose band. Zip is real good about sticking his head right in if you hold it so he can. Watch."

Zip came forward and slid his head neatly between the straps.

"Don't be rough sliding it over the ears. You don't want to cause head shyness by hurting the horse. Snap the throat latch to the cheek strap," I said pointing to the parts.

"Now get your lead and snap it onto the ring beneath his chin. Lead him to the grooming bay."

Todd held his arm out straight to keep Zip at arms length but managed to get him into a bay. I showed him the grooming tools and how to use them, checked on Taylor who was doing a good job, and went to get Roxy's saddle. I talked Taylor through tacking up and walked with him to the arena. I attached the two way radio to his waist band in the small of his back, watched him mount and instructed him to walk around until I returned. Todd, being much slighter and shorter than his older brother, used a step stool to tack up Zip. He dropped the lightweight saddle roughly onto Zip's back and clumsily yanked on the bridle. I made him do it over until he settled the saddle softly and was careful not to bang the bit against the patient horse's teeth.

In the saddle Todd was tense. He was squeezing Zip with his legs and gripping white knuckled on the reins. His whole body was rigid as he held on for dear life.

"Todd, your legs are telling Zip to move forward but you're pulling back on the reins. He doesn't know what you want. Relax your legs. The calves should lie just touching his sides.

Loosen up the reins. That's right. Now just squeeze his sides with your calves."

Zip started off at a walk. "Let your calves quit squeezing. Now look at that pylon off to the left and touch Zips side with just your left calf." Zip bent at his poll and curved smoothly but Todd perceived himself losing his balance and grabbed Zip's barrel with both his legs losing his irons in the process. Zip turned toward me and came to stand in front of me as though asking to be relieved of the moron on his back. I stroked his forehead. I turned him to face the arena so I could watch Taylor.

Taylor sat relaxed on Roxy; his pelvis moving with her, his hands moving to keep contact with her mouth. The ear, shoulder, hip and heel line was consistent and he looked perfectly bored. "Move into a trot, Taylor." They made the transition effortlessly as Taylor went into posting on the proper diagonal.

Although I kept my eyes on Taylor, I said to Todd, "Let your feet dangle and let go of the reins."

I let Taylor circle the arena twice before glancing at Todd. His legs were still wrapped and his hands still clutched the reins.

"Todd, you need to let go."

"What if he takes off?"

"He won't."

"But what if..."

"Todd, I would not ask you to do something that would jeopardize you. You must trust me. I would not put you on a horse that would hurt you. And you must trust Zip."

I took hold of the reins. "Let go, Todd. Let your arms dangle at your side. Shake them loose. Can't do it can you? That's because your legs are still tense. Let them dangle too."

Just as Todd loosened his legs Zip heaved a sigh, shifted his weight to one side. Todd clamped his legs in a vise grip punching Zip's sides with his heels so hard I heard the thump. Zip threw his head up in startled surprise. Todd grabbed the reins. Had I not been holding them, he would have given the horse's mouth a severe yank.

"What just happened, Todd?"

"He was gonna bolt."

"No. You were squeezing so tight, he just gave a sigh of relief when you let your legs relax. Then he shifted to a more comfortable position. Let's try again. Dangle the legs and arms."

Zip's head dropped in relaxation. I slipped the reins over his head out of Todd's reach and held them as I glanced back at Taylor who had a sheen of sweat on his brow.

"Walk your horse, Taylor."

I barely saw the cue. He stilled his seat and squeezed the reins. Roxy obediently, smoothly dropped to a walk. Despite his apparent fatigue, Taylor maintained his balanced seat. I looked back at Todd who was sitting slumped and loose in the saddle.

"That's good, Todd, but sit up straight. Good posture in the saddle is as important as good posture out of saddle. That's right."

I turned my attention back to Taylor. "Trot a few steps and then canter," I instructed. I was pleased with his cues. There was no bouncing, just horse and rider flowing as one.

Todd still sat loose.

"Walk your horse, Taylor."

I turned my attention back to Todd. "Okay Todd, I'm going to walk Zip over to the phone over there. I want you to let your pelvis move with his movement. Keep your hands dangling and DON'T grab him with your legs, okay?"

His mouth was tight but he nodded.

We walked to the phone on the wall and I called for an assistant. Alyssa came in.

"I just need you to walk Zip around the arena, Alyssa. Todd, imagine a steel rod connecting your heel, hip, shoulder, ear and coming out the top of your head. Keep breathing, keep your eyes on the dressage letters along the top of the wall, okay?"

I glanced at Taylor. "You did great Taylor. Cool her out and groom her."

Todd was trying his best to remain relaxed and balanced in the saddle. My plan became to work him on the lunge line for several lessons before I gave him the reins again. After three circles around the arena, I told him he could dismount. I let Alyssa go back to her work and I talked Todd through untacking and grooming Zip once again.

Chapter 12

We couldn't have asked for a better night for our trail ride. Millions of stars twinkled in a clear sky. As the sun went to bed early the temperatures dropped to nose nipping cold. The brightly lit barn rang with laughter as our boarders tacked up. The parking lot was full of horse trailers from across the state. Even those riders called greetings to those they recognized from other trail rides as they saddled and bridled their horses. Dr. Flowers, Jake and Brandi were checking shot records and collecting the participation fee.

A few horses called out to the newcomers and then "Mount up" rang through the air. Horse shoes scraped on cement aisles and clomped on packed dirt. Saddles creaked, bridles jangled, horses played with their bits and shuffled their feet. Their breath misted in the cooling air and looked like chargers going off to war for a noble cause.

We had instructed everyone to pick a partner, preferably someone you didn't know. This was for safety as well as social reasons. Jake led the way on George whom we had discovered was bombproof. His partner was a young woman with another steady horse. We had warned riders about the jack o'lanterns that smiled with internal flickering flame. Many riders were having a hard time getting their horses past them. Some led their horses past and then mounted. A few got on the other side of several Phoenix horses that had been desensitized to the other-worldly expressions. We were all proud of the Phoenix horse composure.

I had to keep an eye on Arielle who partnered up with an older man. I had told Mrs. Adkins I'd watch out for her to convince her Arielle would be safe on the trail ride. Cherry Tart was proving to be a wonderful trail horse. Of course, I made Brandi, Shelly, Russ, Jake, Alyssa and Joe all swear to help.

The Sawyer family had signed up. Luckily we had acquired two more schooling horses. Todd was starting to trust Zip and make progress on his riding. But I was very upset when Marjorie said she wasn't participating on the trail ride. I thought it a bit dishonest since she had signed up and I wasn't planning on having to keep watch over so many. But they all seemed excited, even Todd. I watched in amazement as he tacked up Zip and partnered with another older man in western gear.

I couldn't believe how smoothly the three mile ride went. A few skittish horses took courage from the more steadfast mounts and we all made it to the bonfire area without mishap. The horses were tied to the tether line, cinches were loosened, riders gravitated to the warmth, light and fragrances of the fire. The McMullens had coffee, cider, and hot chocolate brewing. Edibles were hot dogs and marshmallows for roasting; potato, macaroni and jello salads; chips and even chili.

The kids gravitated into a ball that bounced from seats by the fire to the food tables and back again. I kept counting them to be sure they all stayed in the light. I noticed Jake and Mrs. McMullen would join their group for a chat and then leave them again.

Mr. McMullen brought out a guitar and to my surprise Dr. Flowers brought out a fiddle. The kids groaned but soon got into the spirit as Phil McMullen called out a square dance. I was amazed at the number of trail riders that got up to swing their partners. I was enjoying watching the dancers try to draw our kids in.

I heard a horse neigh and thought I'd better check to be sure there was no problem. I heard voices as I walked toward the tether lines.

"Arielle, you go on back. Don't let this happen again. I'd hate for you to get grounded."

I slipped behind a tree and watched silently as Arielle slipped back in the circle of firelight by the food tables.

"She's a pretty lady, isn't she?"

I heard no answer from my place of concealment.

"I'm sure you weren't planning any mischief with her but let me tell you son, hormones are pretty powerful. The mark of a man is being able to control his urges and treat women with respect. You're both smart kids. I'm sure college is in both your futures. Don't ruin your lives with a moment of indiscretion. You get my drift?"

"Yes sir."

I saw Taylor slink back to the group which was now singing Home on the Range. I stepped from behind the tree. He touched his western hat in greeting. "Evenin' ma'am."

"Good evening. Enjoying the trail ride?"

"Sure am. I go to lots of them. I enjoy meeting new people and old friends."

"And playing chaperon?"

"They didn't mean no harm. Just exploring a new social situation."

I laughed. "That's a unique way of putting it. I'm just amazed that my efforts to keep an eye on them all failed."

"You need to enjoy this outing also."

"Thanks for your forgiveness."

"Nothing to forgive."

"I'm Madison Kurt, owner of Phoenix Stables." I held out my hand.

"Pleased to meet you. I'm Jeremiah Johnson." He took mine in a warm clasp.

"You're kidding?"

"Nope. Mom was a real Robert Redford fan and environmentalist. She did her best to be a real mountain woman."

"I didn't know they had T.V. in the mountains," I laughed.

"Well, she had to work in town to support her kids, but if we had to, we could survive in the mountains."

"Where you from?"

"Raised in the Adirondacks of New York. Presently from Union Camp, Indiana."

"That's a' ways."

"Yep."

There was a slight pause as I walked the tether lines making sure all the horses were all right.

"They won't get into any trouble, will they?" he asked.

"No. Thanks again for keeping an eye on the kids."

The horses were fine. Jeremiah took my elbow and guided me back toward the fire. His touch was gentle and sent an electrical shock up my arm and down into my solar plexus.

I worked harder at keeping an eye on the kids. By the time we got back to the barn at ten o'clock, I had a headache. Jeremiah searched me out to say goodbye. "Hope to see you at your next trail ride, ma'am."

Jake sidled up to me as Jeremiah left. "New boyfriend?"

I slid my arm around his waist. "Just a nice guy that helped keep an eye on the kids and caught a couple out in the dark."

"No way! I was trying so hard to watch out for all of them."

We were shutting off the barn lights. The last car was driving down the lane; turning onto the main road.

"I was a bit chagrined myself. I sure am glad he was helping us. Did you see how he mingled and made everyone seem welcome and happy to have come? I might hire him to be here next time," I laughed. "You'll never guess what his name is."

Chapter 13

The fire truck was an old fashion tanker pulled by Zip and Roxy. The bell was ringing. A cartoon Dalmation dog ran alongside barking at the cartoon firemen as they thundered into the parking lot. With one at either end of the teeter-totter pump handles, they pumped the water from the tanker while a bucket brigade worked from the pump at our water trough.

I looked on in horror as the bell kept ringing, horses screamed from inside the burning barn and Jake came running out engulfed in flames. The cartoon characters ignored him and continued their feeble efforts to douse the raging fire as the fire bell kept ringing.

I awoke in a sweat and realized the phone was ringing. Chilled and shivering I answered. "Hello."

"Ms. Kurt? Forgive me for calling so early. This is Melissa Johnson. We've been playing phone tag so long I thought an early morning wake up call might get us a connection."

"It worked. Good thinking."

"I knew a Madison Kurt once. I owe her a great debt for putting me on a horse for the first time in my life."

I gasped. "You're THAT Melissa Johnson?"

"I am. To repay that debt, I'd like to cater your event at cost."

"It isn't going to be a very big event; maybe thirty people. I hear you do killer stuffed crabs and pecan tarts."

"I can certainly put those on the menu. What's the event?"

"A surprise wedding."

"Yours?"

"Yes."

"Congratulations. In that case, let me do it for free as my wedding gift to you. Is there a kitchen where it's going to be held, and what time?"

"My home just outside of Montaine. It starts December 31 at nine o'clock. The actual wedding will take place just after midnight."

"If I can come early, I can cook everything fresh, and clean up after wards. All I ask is a place to take a nap so I'm fresh for serving."

"You've got it. Let me give you directions."

Good feelings of nostalgia occupied my mind when I hung up the receiver. I really wanted to find someone who needed horses in their life and make it a reality. I let my mind wander back to when I gave Melissa her lessons and how riding changed her. I had really enjoyed it and it made me feel I had done something good in both our lives.

It wasn't until much later at the clinic that vague memories of the dream gave me the shivers. Things were going so well in my life. Were they about to change? Or was the dream just a warning to check the wiring at the barn. I called Jake immediately and suggested it.

"We did that first thing, honey," he reminded me.

"Oh, I'd forgotten."

"What brought this on?"

I told him of the dream.

"The cartoon characters mean it isn't real. The fire just means we're hot stuff," Jake chuckled.

"Then I wouldn't have felt horrified. Things are so idyllic right now. I'm so afraid the bubble is about to burst."

"Madison, you've paid your dues with lots of hard decisions and work. You deserve this satisfying life. And I want to be a part of it."

"Oh, Jake, you are part of it. I'm glad we're getting married in January instead of next Fall."

"Me too."

"Speaking of...the caterer I've been playing phone tag with, called me at five thirty this morning."

"Ouch, that's kind of early."

"Well, at least we finally connected. Remember Melissa Johnson that I gave lessons to twelve or thirteen years ago?"

"You're kidding?"

"Not kidding. She's going to cater our wedding for free just because I gave her those lessons."

"See. You're blessed. And I'm blessed to be marrying you."

I no sooner hung up the phone and was headed into the number three examining room when Dr. Flowers came out of number two. "Oh, Madison, we need to talk after we close."

"Something wrong?"

"Depends on how you look at it. Nothing that can't be fixed. Nothing to worry about."

I didn't have time to worry, actually. The after noon was booked solid and we squeezed in two walk in emergencies as well. It was going on seven o'clock when we thanked our receptionist, Jennifer, for staying over and locked up. We poured ourselves the last of the coffee. I cleaned the coffee machine and pot while Clint gathered his thoughts.

"Madison, I've changed my mind about retiring. Since you've come our business has increased. But neither do I want to continue working so many hours. What I'd really like to do is start a western saddle club for youngsters. Phil McMullen is interested in helping with the project. I'd like to base it at Phoenix."

My mouth was hanging open. He hurried on before I could close it.

"I'm thinking you don't need to increase your hours here at the clinic with the farm claiming so much of your energy. Maybe you'll even need to cut down. So how about we take on another partner. Can you afford to share the wealth?"

"Yes! I love your saddle club idea. I'll build another indoor arena so we can add more activities and the boarders will still have access to the present riding arena. And how about an outside arena for pole bending, barrel racing and western shows."

"Boy, you're way ahead of me. I'd like to offer lessons as incentives for troubled kids to improve school grades. Would that worry you?"

"Not as long as you take responsibility for them. I think Jake would really love to help with that kind of project."

"There's a young man on the police force that's interested as well. He'll be a good resource for finding those troubled kids. Will we need to hire two new doctors? Sounds like you might have to devote full time to Phoenix."

"Shelly is doing a great job of managing the farm so I don't think I'm ready to quit yet."

"Good, but once the new guy is here we can cut back a bit. You know, new stables and arenas will take up a good portion of your pastures and fields. I just heard there's a parcel of farm land for sale down the road from you. I think I'll check into it. We can use it for growing our own hay and oats which will give us lots of straw."

"Listen to us grow."

Chapter 14

Both of the new schooling horses we had purchased just before Halloween were Hanoverians that made my heart tingle with nostalgia and missing Fritz. Parcheesi was in his prime and had been a winning dressage competitor who suddenly decided he was unworthy of first place ribbons. I suspected he was just bored with dressage. I would be working him in cross country as long as the weather held, and in arena jumping when it got too cold. Hopefully, after a break from dressage, he would regain his enthusiasm for it and could be used as a three day eventer.

Casablanca Knight had been used in arena jumping. He was past his prime but would be good for starting beginner and intermediate students in jumping.

The Sawyer children were all doing well on their mounts. It was time to assess and move them to new mounts as our number of students at all levels was increasing.

Lori's enthusiasm for riding made me eager to ask of her equestrian goals. When I asked where she wanted to go with her riding she replied, "As far as I can."

She was doing great on Argo but I specifically had her in mind for Parcheesi's competition teammate and I wanted Brandi to mentor her. I needed to get Parcheesi ready in cross country and show jumping first. Until then, with her mom's permission, we put her with Casablanca Knight to work on her own jumping skills.

I asked Lisa what her riding goals were. "To make it to age nineteen and into college without any broken bones."

I laughed. "Smart goals but wouldn't you enjoy it if you had to think and participate more in riding?"

"No. I like Deek. We're good together."

"You're both sleeping through the lesson. I'll make you a deal. You improve his performance and I'll leave the two of you together. If that isn't possible, I'm going to switch you to George."

"George looks harmless enough."

"Only if he respects you. So George it is."

Lisa looked a bit worried when she left that Friday.

I contacted the construction company on Monday. They were booked until after Thanksgiving. I said that was fine. It would give me time to lay out the area I wanted them to use for the new arena and stable. For now, we had enough stalls for Dr. Flowers to start looking for Saddle Club mounts. Eventually, however, they'd be moved to the new stable area. We warned Shelly of the expansion plans and gave her the go ahead to start interviewing for two more stable hands.

On Tuesday, Taylor and Todd came as usual. "Todd, I want you to ride Roxy today."

The familiar thin lips and furrowed brow appeared. "Why?"

"Because you've really progressed on Zip. You've been taking part in lessons; not just sitting on his back. I want to see you doing the same on Roxy."

"But I trust Zip."

"You need to know you can handle other horses as well. Besides, I have new students starting. I need Zip for the very beginning beginners."

"Which one will I ride then?" asked Taylor as Todd went off to groom and tack up Roxy.

"Which one do you want to ride?"

He shuffled his feet and looked down. "Am I good enough for Knight?" It was almost a whisper.

"Actually yes."

He looked up in surprise.

"You won't be going over four footers for a while but I think the two of you will get on well. Are you that interested in riding or competing?"

"No, but if I have to ride I'd like it to be a bit more interesting."

"Understood. Make sure you pick up a consent form for your mom to sign before you leave. Go ahead and ride Knight. Start getting to know him."

Arielle had shown up one weekend carrying her report card and wearing a grin. She had straight A's. "Awesome, Arielle."

"So can I pick up another night here at the stables?"

"What do your parents say?"

"It's okay as long as my grades don't drop."

"How is Cherry Tart doing?"

"Good. I ride every night between school and homework. She gets the weekend off. Dad has made us an outdoor arena with rubber footing. We do endurance work through the fields as well as working on dressage in the arena."

"What happens when you pick up another night?"

"She'll get Wednesdays off. Maybe I'll work her on an occasional Saturday or Sunday."

"Wednesday is a good day to be at the stable. Some boarders skip coming. You might be able to pick up some extra money lunging or grooming some extra horses. Her brown eyes sparkled. "And since you're off this Friday for Thanksgiving weekend, how about I come out and show you some new dressage maneuvers?"

"I've been watching Georgeann on Buick, and practicing on Cherry."

"Good role model to watch. I'll check out how you're doing. Maybe you'll get enough points this next show season to move up pretty fast."

"I hope so. Madison?"

"Yes?"

"There's this girl at school. She really loves horses but all the money goes to pay for her older sister's college tuition..."

I smiled. "Can you get her and her parents to visit the stables?"

"Arielle smiled back. "I'll sure try, for Darla's sake."

With as busy as the Phoenix was I barely had time to think about my wedding. I woke up one morning in a panic wondering what I had left undone. I sat down and made a list: Dress... check, caterer...check, bouquet, boutonniere...check. Looked like we still needed a photographer. I grabbed the phone book and made a list of photographers. On lunch break, I started calling. By the end of the list, I still had no photographer. They were all booked. I informed Jake that evening about the dilemma.

"Let me ask around some of my clients. Maybe we can still find one in time. If all else fails we can let Marshall in on the secret. Photography is his hobby."

I sighed with relief.

The day before Thanksgiving our last stall was leased. I gave another sigh of relief. I also approached Georgeann about mentoring Arielle and got quite a shock.

"She's welcome to watch all she wants," Georgeann said coldly, "but I don't have time to help a competitor take away my ribbons."

"Oh Georgeann, I'm sure she's a far ways from taking any of your titles."

"No matter. I did it on my own. She can do it on her own. It's character building."

"Well, thanks for sharing your views."

I had to chuckle to myself thinking of how it had built her character. The chuckle died a quick death, however, at the reality of it. So many people grow up bitter for lack of a little encouragement or opportunity. It made me even more determined to share horses with as many as I could and encourage them all.

Chapter 15

We closed the clinic for the four days over Thanksgiving weekend. Dr. Flowers and I split the emergency "on call" shifts.

I actually attempted a small turkey with lots of help from Jake. We played scrabble with Clint and Shelly. After dinner Jake wouldn't let me clear up. About an hour later a young lady arrived and did it. Jake was all grins at gifting me with the kitchen help. Or maybe he didn't want to have to help. Either way, I was impressed with Angie's quiet manner and efficient work. I asked if she was interested in a permanent job as housekeeper and part time cook. She was thrilled. I was thrilled. Jake was thrilled. I saw him give her a wink and wondered if she was a client needing a job. I invited her to join us for an evening of relaxation and watching Miracle on 34th St.

I was able to go visit Arielle and Cherry Tart on Friday morning. She astounded me with what she had picked up from Georgeann and implemented with Cherry Tart. The girl definitely had a gift for training horses. I was feeling strongly that she needed to make it her life's work.

"Arielle, you have such a gift with horses. I think it's time to switch your duties to riding and training. We'll have to pass your stall work onto someone else."

Arielle's eyes gleamed. "You mean it?"

"I sure do. Let's hope your friend Darla is interested in working for lessons. Oh, you'll have to get permission from your parents."

"Oh, thank you, Madison."

"In fact, I think if Darla comes, you can be her trainer in her barn duties and her riding instructor. Think you can do that?"

"Awesome."

"Besides that, how would you like to learn jumping?"

"Oh, yes!"

"Ask your parents. You can start riding C.K."

I gave Arielle a ride to the Phoenix. Her parents said they'd pick her up at seven and would sign the permission slips then. I could see the surprise and a glimmer of pride in their eyes.

As we pulled into the parking lot, Arielle squealed, "There's Darla."

I glanced ahead and saw Shelly talking with a family of dark skin. The family of horse lovers knows no bounds, I thought. But the tightness of Shelly's face created a knot in my stomach.

As we parked, Arielle leaped from the car and ran to Darla who smiled a small smile at her friend. Shelly pointed at me and the parents looked my way. They didn't look happy either. I stuck out my hand. "Hello. I'm Madison Kurt."

The man shook my hand. "Hello. I'm Franklin Lee. This is my wife Emma and my daughter Darla."

"Emma, Darla." I shook each of their hands and noted the mother's clasp was weak but Darla's was a bit stronger. "I hear Darla wants to be a horsewoman."

"I think maybe it isn't a good idea," said the father.

"Why is that?"

"You might lose some boarders. I won't have my daughter blamed for that, nor do I want her subjected to discrimination."

"With all due respect, Mr. Lee, I'm sure Darla has already confronted discrimination. Unfortunately she may have to throughout her life. I would hope she'll not let it keep her from going for what she wants."

I was thinking to myself that she probably got it from both races as her skin color was a pale chocolate color. Both parents were fairly light.

"As far as losing boarders, so be it. I'll not foster discrimination by choosing a boarder over someone willing to work for her dreams. I'm sure the stalls won't remain empty for long."

"You're very optimistic young lady. But you might be surprised at the consequences of allowing Darla to ride."

"As long as she's willing to work for the lessons, I'll take that chance."

"Excuse me? My daughter doesn't do menial labor," interjected Emma.

"Mrs. Lee, a sure way to see if someone is a true horse lover is to see if they're willing to care for them. Knowing about cleanliness in the barn, first aid, nutrition and grooming is all part of being a horsewoman."

I turned to Darla. "Darla, are you willing to learn from the ground up?"

She solemnly nodded her head. It looked like she was trying hard not to let the hope bubble to the surface. She looked to her father. "Please, Daddy?"

"Before you say yes, I must warn you, Mr. Lee, that riding and working around horses is inherently dangerous."

Mr. Lee was hesitating.

"Daddy, I can get hurt riding in a car, playing soccer, or even just going to school. Pleeease. I really want to do this."

Franklin looked at me. "Ms. Kurt, if you are willing to lose customers to accommodate my daughter, I can do no less than give her the chance to explore her dream."

"Done! Shelly will get you the forms to fill out. Darla, Arielle will be your trainer and instructor. I expect her to expect your best. Can you handle that?"

"Yes, ma'am."

"Arielle, wait until the forms are signed and then show them around, okay?"

I turned to head for the stalls. My peripheral vision saw Jake getting out of his car, Mrs. Ley waving from hers and Cindy in riding breeches and boots skipping toward the huge sliding doors that were open only about three feet to keep out the excess cold. I was focused, however, on Georgeann. She had been standing with fists on hips in the doorway. When Darla and Arielle had danced a jig of joy she had abruptly swung inside, her blond bun bobbing like the musical bouncing ball. I was sure she was a lost customer.

I was on my way to deal with her and passed Cindy who was standing head to head with the newest horse stabled in stall eleven. It was nothing unusual to see her communicating with the horses. It always fascinated me and I'd stop to watch and learn about the horse. But this time I had a crisis to deal with and so paid no heed when I hear her say "home".

"Georgeann, is something wrong? You seem upset."

"If you're going to allow nnn...them here, I'll be leaving."

"That's your prerogative, but yes, I believe anyone with a love of horses has a right to learn to care for and ride them."

"Mucking stalls is fine but wearing breeches is not for the lower classes."

I laughed. "I'm sure you consider me a lower class than yourself."

"Well, you descended from Burnadette Kurt and you own Phoenix. I must say I'm sorry to see you taking steps to allow it to degrade so soon."

It was the first time I'd heard myself held in such high regard because of my pedigree. Mom would have been thrilled.

I heard metal snapping and thumping against wood. A horse snorted and shuffled his feet. I glanced back in time to see the stall guard drop from in front of the new horse. "Cindy, NO!"

It was too late. My shout startled her. She jumped with a look of consternation on her face. The horse bolted from the stall spinning Cindy around with her arms out wide. I ran for her but shouted "SHUT THE DOOR," not even knowing if anyone would hear.

Miraculously the patch of sky showing beyond the doors shrank to a crack and disappeared completely. The horse sat on his haunches and slid, the shoes throwing sparks from metal on cement. He threw back his head to keep from hitting the closed doors and went over backward. He scrambled up leaving blood from scraped hocks on the floor.

"Are you okay, Cindy?" I wondered if the dark spot on her forehead was a bruise.

"Hurt?" She tried to go to the horse that was trotting in circles looking for an escape.

Was she speaking of herself hurt or the horse? "You can't turn horses loose, Cindy."

She stomped her foot, crossed her arms and scowled, furrowing the shadowed spot. "Home. Horsey go home."

"This is his home now."

"No. Horsey go home. He's lost."

Jake had opened the door enough to slip through. Mrs. Ley was rushing toward us and Jake crooned to the horse until he could put his hands on him. With Cindy safely in her mother's arms, I grabbed the horse's halter from its peg and slowly approached them.

"Madison, what's on this horse?"

I reached forward to touch the horse. Its winter coat felt stiff as if with hair gel. I stroked him and talked softly. When

I pulled my hand away it was smudged with brown and perfectly matched the shadowed spot on Cindy's forehead.

Just then, Joe brought in a horse from the arena. "Joe, have you groomed this horse since it's been here?" Jake asked as we led it back to his stall.

"Nope. Orders are to feed and turn out. Nothing else. The guy said it's a mean bugger and he doesn't want anyone to get hurt."

Jake and I looked at each other and at the horse walking calmly between us. "Well, it doesn't look mean. Can you clean those scrapes on his hocks and put on some antibiotic salve?"

"You bet. There's shoe polish all over him. Okay to go ahead and bathe that off of him?"

"Yes."

Mrs. Ley apologized for Cindy's jail break.

Jake turned his attention to the child. "Ready to ride, Cindy?"

She nodded her head and took Jake's hand as they headed for our wing.

Arielle arrived with the Lees and Georgeann made a point to throw something to emphasize her displeasure as she left. I put my hand on Emma's arm and threw in a wink for good measure. "Not to worry. Those kind of characters we can do without."

On my way to Shelly's office, I wondered about Cindy's sureness of the horse being lost and needing to go home. "Shelly, what can you tell me about the horse in stall eleven?"

She pulled her rolodex toward her. "Name is Maple Syrup, Quarter Horse, fifteen, two hands. Dark brown with two hind socks. Owner is Joshua Crable. Just here until he gets his barn built in Pennsylvania. Don't groom. Just feed and turn out. Claims the horse is too mean and he doesn't want anyone to get hurt."

"Have you been around the horse?"

"Yep. Not a mean bone in his body."

"Doesn't that strike you as odd?"

"No more than the brown stiff stuff all over his body. I've called the police to see if anyone has reported a missing or stolen horse. Joe alerted me to the fact that he wasn't mean and had coloring on him. I was going to tell you but didn't think I should in front of the Lees, and then you were dealing with Georgeann."

I smiled. "I knew there was a reason I hired you as barn manager. Thanks Shelly. Keep me posted."

"Should we give the horse a bath or act like we don't suspect anything?"

"We already gave Joe the go ahead with that. Didn't want the stuff to get in the lacerations and infect it. Joshua Crable will know we're suspicious if he comes around but it can't be helped. Hopefully the police will be here before his is."

"I wouldn't worry about that, he hasn't been here since he brought the horse and paid three months rent."

"This is getting deeper by the moment. If he does come around, don't let him take the horse from the premises."

"Got 'cha."

Chapter 16

Clint Flowers was interviewing new graduates once again but surprised me with showing me a resume from an established small animal veterinarian from Georgia. We both wondered why he'd close his facility to start over, but we liked the looks of the resume.

We were at the clinic interviewing on the Saturday after Thanksgiving. Shelly called to let me know Maple Syrup was actually Buffalo Head Penny. The police had called and then brought a Brickfield family including a distraught young woman. Sheri brought a picture of her missing horse. Now that Maple Syrup had had a bath he was a deep golden palomino and was a perfect duplicate of the horse in the picture. They also had registration papers showing the matching markings.

Sheri went to the field and yelled for "Buufff." The horse's head shot up from grazing, whinnied to his real owner and returned to her at a gallop which set the other horses in the pasture to running and kicking up their heels. There was no question in any mind present who the horse belonged to.

Shelly described Joshua Crable to Sheri and the police. He was actually Rick Stimmel, Sheri's ex-boyfriend who had been threatening to get even since Sheri broke up with him. He was attending a college in the next state. Mr. and Mrs. Brickfield said they would press charges. The police left to put out a warrant for his arrest.

"Let us know when you find him. We owe him two months rent refund."

"I wouldn't worry about it," one of the policemen said.

Shelly insisted, however. "He might need it for legal fees."

"Why are you siding with him?" asked Mrs. Brickfield.

"I'm not siding with him. The money rightfully belongs to him. He paid for three months rent. The horse wasn't even here a month."

"He's a thief."

"That doesn't mean I must be one."

Shelly filled me in on all that had transpired and then ended by saying Georgeann had loaded Buick and left right behind the Brickfields. "I wouldn't worry, though, Madison. Word gets around. We already have a waiting list. I'll be making phone calls. The stalls will be filled in no time."

"I didn't know we had a waiting list."

"I wanted to give you the list as a Christmas gift, but I guess you need it now as a pat on the back for standing up for Darla and returning Rick's money."

"You did that."

"But you backed me up and you're the boss."

"I wasn't really worried but I am thrilled we have a waiting list. Wait; was Joshua Crable on the waiting list?"

"Afraid so. I guess that makes it premeditated horse stealing doesn't it? Does that make me an accomplice?"

"I sure hope not. I'd hate to lose you, Shelly." We both laughed.

Putting my attention back to the interviews, Clint really liked two of them. Mark McCorrmack and Vicki Torrence were both graduating in the spring. Clint said he'd accept whoever took the position first. Both had spouses to consult. We had our fingers crossed that the Georgia man, Conner Winston, would be acceptable and could start sooner. His interview was the following Wednesday.

He was about five feet, ten inches tall with light brown hair and green eyes. He had laugh creases at the corners of his eyes but his eyes claimed they hadn't laughed in awhile. He spoke with assurance in his knowledge, and gentleness in his hands. Clint and I both liked him immediately and hired him on the spot. Clint hesitated to inform the other applicants of our choice.

"I think we might need another large animal vet. The horses seem to be coming out of the woodwork," he said. I knew Conner wasn't interested in vetting the big animals. We had said that was fine. I thought I could handle the growing number of horses in the community that were privately owned or boarded at Phoenix; at least for now. Maybe by spring graduation, we would need another veterinarian.

I invited Conner and Clint to my place to have dinner with Jake and I. I called Angie to warn her of the company for dinner. Despite the short notice she had a wonderful pasta meal prepared and even surprised us with seafood appetizers. I invited Angie to join us as we ate and socialized.

Conner refused the offer of vacation time between jobs other than time to move. He'd leave in the morning to gather his things and make arrangements to transport his belongings. He had found an apartment before he arrived at my place.

We enjoyed an evening of getting to know each other but we resisted the question that was most on our minds.

Five days after Thanksgiving it snowed a light dusting of icy crystals. The foundation and shell of the new arena was up. I urged them to put up the stable shell next so they could then work inside on both of them.

Clint had purchased the first saddle club mount. He was a buckskin quarter horse named Zip Lock. He turned out to be Spiffy Zip's full brother and was just as mellow although a few years younger. Clint brought Zip Lock and stabled him in our wing Friday after clinic hours. Conner came along to visit the stable area of Phoenix.

We were explaining the relationship between the two brothers as Cindy was riding Zip. Horse and rider came to where we were standing. Zip stretched out his muzzle to Conner's hand which was making its way toward the horse. Cindy smiled and shook her head "yes".

"Yes, what, Cindy?" I asked.

She just giggled and the duo turned to enter their own world again.

"What was that about?" asked Conner.

"I think you passed the Cindy Ley seal of approval."

"That's a good thing, I hope."

"A very good thing," I said as I watched Shelly collide with a doorframe while her eyes were on Conner. The thud made the fellas turn to look. While all they saw was a red faced Shelly backing away from the frame and disappearing though the door, I was chuckling under my breath and hoping it would be a match.

Conner liked the Saddle Mount club idea and said to count him in where ever he could be of help. He was taking the majority of the clinic hours which freed up Clint and me for our Phoenix activities and responsibilities. That alone, was a great help.

Brandi, Shelly, Jake and I were all giving lessons. Arielle was teaching Darla. I was impressed with her results. I wanted desperately to increase her work schedule and resulting paycheck but I didn't dare jeopardize her school grades. Summer would be soon enough.

Cindy refused to ride Zip one night insisting Zip was tired. She chose Deek and surprised us all with her expertise in handling him as well as his response to her. We trailered Zip to Phil's place for a rest.

Lisa really started to improve on George. I harbored a secret hope I could get her to compete on him, at least in Hunter Under Saddle. Lori, Arielle, and Taylor were all enjoying jumping on Casablanca Knight. I'd soon need another jumper for them to improve on. Then I would have C.K. for beginners moving up in their horsemanship skills. Todd was moved to Deek and surprised himself with the ease with which he handled him. As his confidence increased, his reluctance to being at Phoenix was disappearing.

There were several new students at various levels and all our horses were in use. Parcheesie was the only horse I was working. He took readily to cross country and his first efforts over small arena jumps since the snow forced us indoors had his intense interest.

We had lost no more boarders because of Darla's presence and the last two stalls were rented within a week of Georgeann, Buick, and Buffalo Head Penny leaving. All was well at Phoenix. I had a satisfaction that had eluded my mother and I felt sad that she had never attained what she had longed for.

During the first week of December Jake and I took an afternoon off to Christmas shop, go out to dinner, plan a Christmas party for the weekend before Christmas, and enjoy a quiet evening. When he left to go home, I felt an emptiness. I realized how much he resembled my father. Quiet, fun, encouraging. I was sure marriage to Jake was all I needed for my life to be complete. I could hardly wait.

Chapter 17

Although the top of the bank barn was used for hay and straw storage, we had renovated the bottom after a good cleaning, with insulation, a ceiling and floor, rest rooms and lots of lights. It would be our party place. Our mailing list included the participants near and far, of our first trail ride, our boarders, students and their families, and those on our waiting list. I even invited Melissa Johnson.

Before Mr. Ballard bought the place it had been a dairy farm. The bank barn was quite huge. We were thankful for that. It would handle the mass of people even if everyone showed up with their required covered dish. We were supplying drinks and eating utensils.

We had a much smaller Christmas party for all our employees the Thursday before the big one. They got Christmas bonuses and offers of double time to help with the big party. All ten agreed.

And then it began to snow.

Despite the short notice and continual snow, the turn out for our party was commendable. Shelly looked stunning in a red dress with tiny scintillating sparkles all over it. Clint brought and introduced the young police officer he had mentioned. John Smith joked he was looking for Pocahontas and went to talk to Shelly.

Melissa showed up with her daughter Chelsea. Chelsea was rail thin and wore the glum look of a teen who hadn't discovered herself yet. Melissa apologized to me saying her daughter hadn't wanted to come. She had forced her hoping the horses might affect her the way they had affected herself at that age.

Alyssa was on to Chelsea in a flash, taking her to get a drink, introducing her to the other teens and any adult who passed close. A smile would flash on Chelsea's face for an instant but would disappear as soon as the other person moved on. Joe soon had her out on the dance floor.

Mrs. Ley was there helping arrange food and attending the CD player with the music selections. She said she was repaying the debt of us taking the chance of allowing Cindy to come to the stables. She was trying to also keep an eye on her waif of a child. Even though Cindy had come a long way socially, she was still prone to seeking out the horses rather than people. Although Gloria thought it a huge debt to pay, I thought Cindy's connection with the horses invaluable. She often let us know when a horse was tired, unhappy with tack, needed a break, didn't like a particular student or, I thought ruefully, was lost and needed to go home.

Conner came with the "on call" pager and Jeremiah Johnson followed. He came straight to us to thank us for the invitation and then started socializing throughout the room. He must have danced with every woman there by the end of the evening, including Darla, Cindy Ley and myself. I gave him credit for making the party a success with his gregariousness.

Russ and Brandi brought Daryl and his girl friend, Megan.

"What, no karaoke?" he scoffed.

"I promise to have a competition with our next year's party," I laughed.

Santa made an appearance. He had discounts for visitors and students, hoof picks for young boarders and mane and tail detangler for adult boarders.

I saw Arielle speaking and dancing with Taylor. Socializing was part of their duties to make sure everyone was involved and had a good time. To her credit, she didn't let him keep her from circulating to fill drinks, pass desserts or encourage wall flowers to mingle.

When I saw a pause in her activities I approached her. "Arielle, I'll bet you aren't riding Cherry in this weather are you?"

She laughed. "No. She'll get a break until spring."

"If you want, why not move her to Phoenix. You can ride the bus here from school. I'm sure one of the other grooms can drive you home in the Phoenix truck. I really want you to be ready in March and you can start her over jumps if you want."

"Oh WOW. Thanks a lot Madison."

"Merry Christmas."

"Ready for what?" asked Jeremiah.

"Showing in dressage and maybe starting in three day evening. You should see the training she's done with her horse. Arielle is a natural trainer."

"That's great. Will you make it your life's work?"

"That would be great but mom and dad are insisting I go to college."

"That's a wise idea but there are schools where you take your horse along," I informed her.

"That would be so awesome."

"Well, I'm sure I don't have to remind you to keep up your grades."

"I sure will."

"You know," interjected Jeremiah, "sometimes you'll find life's day job is something else and training turns out to be an avocation. It's okay either way."

"I can't imagine wanting to do anything else."

"That's your first guidepost," I added.

Arielle nodded and moved to help a child trying to carry a plate of food and balance a drink as well. Jeremiah took my elbow and guided me toward the tables of food.

"I haven't seen you eat. You're too busy trying to make sure everyone is having a good time. Are you hungry?"

"Are you watching me that close?"

"As a matter of fact, I am. If Jake ever leaves the picture, I plan to be there to fill in the hole."

He handed me a red paper plate and a green napkin.

"That's an awfully large hole to fill."

"At first it would be, but time has a way of filling in the edges a bit."

I was a bit stunned by his bluntness and the way he was putting various foods on my plate without regard for what I might choose.

He continued. "Phoenix seems to be a growing enterprise. When are you going to narrow your activities? Hours at the clinic must drag compared to being here?"

"Not so," I retorted. "I enjoy being a veterinarian. Phoenix has an awesome barn manager. I feel quite comfortable going to the clinic knowing Phoenix is in her capable hands."

"That would be Shelly, right?"

"That would be."

"She's a pretty woman...sparkling tonight," he grinned.

"In more ways than one."

"One day, she'll marry and move on."

"I'll deal with that when it happens."

He chuckled. "You're quite a woman, Madison. Facing Life head on...never cowering."

"How would you know that? How would you know any of this?"

"From your speech and manner. And I make it my business to know what I want to know. Enjoy your evening."

Jeremiah walked away from me to Shelly and swept her out on the dance floor.

Suddenly I shivered. Was his conviviality strictly social or was there a more sinister motive behind it?

Jake materialized at my side. "Are you okay?"

"Yeah."

"I was on my way over here to punch him out for messing with my woman but he saw me coming."

I smiled. "I'm glad he's scared of you."

"Oh, I don't know about that," he laughed. "He's bigger than I am."

"You're a bigger man than he'll ever be," I stated and then gave him a quick kiss.

The food was devoured, the adults were tired, the young people were slowing down. A few couples left and the women came back in to huddle by the door. Jake and I went to see what was going on. The cars were buried in snow and the husbands were busy clearing windshields and helping each other get unstuck. Jake grabbed his coat and told them to go in to warm up until he got the parking lot cleared. He brought out the tractor with the snow blade and set to work clearing the wet, heavy drifts.

The people poured out of the party hall and good naturedly helped each other rock the cars over the plow wakes. Calling good-byes they fish tailed down the drive. I was concerned about Melissa driving all the way back to Damascus and asked if she'd like to spend the night.

"Do you mind? I really am nervous about the drive."

"I wouldn't have asked if I minded."

Shelly said she was letting the stable help sleep at her place so they wouldn't have to drive home after cleaning up. She asked Chelsea if she wanted to join the clean up group. The girl shrugged her shoulders like it made no difference to her but headed back in to the party hall without consulting her mother. Melissa just smiled.

Jake had put away the tractor and blade. I wrapped my arm around his. "Come in and warm up."

"I'd better get on the road."

"Spend the night."

He kissed me. "Better not. I want the white gown to be legitimate."

"Melissa is spending the night. She'll chaperone. You can sack out on the couch. By morning the salt trucks and plows will have the roads clear. Please?"

"Why?" he grinned, thinking I had ulterior motives.

"I'd just feel better. I won't bother you. I'm going to take a shower and go right to bed. I have to go to the clinic early."

He was still asleep when I kissed him on the cheek. It was dark.

"Madison, NO," he protested.

"Silly. It's five A.M. Coffee is on. By the time you shower your eggs will be ready. You can head for home after you eat. Say, you aren't afraid of sex are you?"

"I'm not falling for that line," he said grinning.

The bacon was in the warmer. I waited until I heard him come out of the upstairs bathroom before I cracked the eggs into the frying pan, pushed down the toaster lever and poured his coffee. He came into the kitchen with a smooth jaw, smelling of soap and with a smile. He came to me and gave me a kiss.

"Smells good Mrs. Andrews."

"We aren't married yet, but I love it when you talk domestic to me."

He laughed. "Just two more weeks."

"I can't wait. Have you found a photographer?"

"I had to let Marshall in on the secret. He'll do the pictures."

"That's great." I paused. "Jake, am I getting carried away with freebies? You'll stop me if I am, won't you?"

"You didn't give Phoenix to Jeremiah did you?" he exclaimed in mock horror.

I smiled meekly. "No, but I offered a free stall for Arielle's Cherry Tart so she can continue preparing for the show circuit. She wants to try jumping to see if she can make her into a three day eventer. And what of the saddle club? Where are we going to get the money to cover that expense? I don't think Clint can finance the whole thing."

"What about a government grant?"

"I don't want government restrictions. We're hoping to help kids before they're in trouble."

"What about expanding? All three wings of the stable have room to add several stalls."

"Do you think they'd fill up right away?"

"Didn't Shelly say we have a waiting list?"

"Yes she did."

"And once the shows start with riders representing us, we'll be attracting more of the show level boarders. Besides, if we fail, we still have our day jobs."

I laughed. "Always the positive force, aren't you."

We kissed and Jake left under a moon peeking from behind thunderclouds promising more snow. The tree branches and split rails surrounding the parking lot still carried a load of the heavy snow resisting the warming temperatures.

Melissa soon came down the stairs. I made her breakfast as she chatted and filled me in on her life that followed the course of college, marriage, baby, divorce. Her catering business was doing well but didn't leave much time for horses. She didn't really mind that but she wished she could get Chelsea involved. Unfortunately Chelsea didn't want to muck stalls or groom dirty horses.

"Well, horses aren't for everyone, Melissa. What about sports, swimming, a musical instrument, or even cake decorating? Maybe she just needs some more time with Mom."

"Yes, that could be true," Melissa sighed.

"The lights are coming on in the barn. Shall we go see if Chelsea changed her mind? Maybe she'll decide horses are cool to be around."

We saw Shelly coming down the stairs from the apartment over the garage.

"Did everyone sleep good?"

The dark circles under her eyes made mockery of the question.

"We managed," she answered evasively.

I glanced at Melissa. The worried look claimed she knew something was wrong. We entered the side door of the stable. There was no usual banter between the stable hands as they fed and scrubbed water buckets. Chelsea sat just inside on a bench with arms crossed and a scowl on her face.

When she saw her mother she jumped to her feet and growled, "Where have you been? Let's get out of here!"

Melissa turned pleading eyes toward me and mouthed "I'm sorry," as her daughter stomped out and slammed the door behind her.

I touched her arm and said, "Don't worry about it. Drive carefully. See you at our New Year's eve party."

She smiled and winked at me. "Wouldn't miss it for the world."

I turned to Shelly. "What happened?"

"She didn't want to help clean up, which was fine. Kept bad mouthing the barn smell, which, of course, was non existent in the social hall. We could excuse that. But she just wanted to hang on the guys. Even woke one up by getting overly close repeatedly. For a moment I thought I'd have to bring her to the house."

"That is one disturbed youngster."

"You got that right."

The cheerful chatter of the stable hands was starting to fill the air now that the trouble maker was gone. I inhaled deeply of the equine aroma before heading out into the warming temperatures already starting to melt the snow. I guiltily thought I was glad Melissa and her wayward child lived two hours away. She was definitely not a candidate for horse therapy. I knew if they lived close, Melissa would want me to try. I would try and probably fail.

It got me to wondering about the saddle club. As the tires hissed on the wet pavement, my mind steamed with doubts. Had my need to mix horses and people gotten me in over my head? I needed to talk to Clint about it.

Chapter 18

One of the first patients of the day was Congo, a German shepherd...and his master John Smith.

"Good morning John."

"Good morning Madison."

"Hello there, Congo. What do you need today?"

"He needs his shots updated."

I ruffed the dog's neck while I looked at his eyes and nose for discharge of any kind. I gently stroked his ears and then held one as I pointed the otoscope deep inside. "What a good boy," I praised as I moved to the other side. I listened to heart and lungs; felt his muscle tone on sides and back legs. "He's in good shape."

"I work him a lot. He has passed his K-9 corp specs and has his tracking certificate. I'm trying to convince the city of Montaine that it would be beneficial to have a Police K-9 corp."

"That might be a hard sell for such a small town."

"I'd settle for allowing us to be a squad of two."

"I'd vote for that."

"Well, thanks for your support."

"Speaking of support, I heard you were going to refer kids for Clint's Saddle club."

"Yeah. I've got about six boys in mind that could use some male authority figures in their lives to give some guidance. I wouldn't mind helping with it as well. I rode as a kid. I'm on the waiting list to board at Phoenix. I've been casually looking for a horse but don't want to jump the gun before you have a stall available."

"Start looking in earnest. You can board in our wing until the saddle club stables are intact. They're making a lot of progress on them. I think Clint is claiming Zip Lock as his mount isn't he?"

"Yes. Looking at Zip Lock and Spiffy Zip, I'd say it's a good line"

The assistant brought in the injections. The dog remained calm as I picked up the loose skin of his neck and injected the immunizations. "You're all set Congo." Looking back at John, I added, "Will we see you at the New Year's eve party?'

"No, I'm scheduled to work. But if you make enough noise, maybe a neighbor will report you and I can stop in to tell you to quiet down.'

I laughed. "I'll see what I can do, but as the nearest neighbor is two miles in any direction, I don't think it will happen."

Just before noon a city worker came into the clinic carrying a limp dog. "Hit him with the salt truck," he sobbed. "Can you save him?"

The dog had tags which I slipped off and handed to our receptionist. "Call the owner, Sue. See what they say."

"I don't care what they say," shouted the grizzled man with tears trickling down his stubbled cheeks. "I'll pay for it.'

Conner kept the clients flowing as Clint and I examined the dog. Sue came back and whispered that "the owner won't pay for anything as the stupid dog keeps getting loose. I told him he had to come immediately to sign a release or the police would charge him with animal abuse."

I smiled at her fast thinking. I went to the man who had brought the dog in. "Sir, the owner doesn't want the dog. I have to warn you, he has less than a fifty percent chance of making it and surgery will cost at least a thousand dollars."

"I've got my credit card with me. I'll put that much up front and pay whatever else is needed."

My heart warmed at the kindness of the man. "We're stabilizing him for now until the owner gets here to release ownership."

"Start now. It might be crucial!" He pulled the visa card from his wallet. "Here run it through for the grand. I have to get back to work. I'll stop in about five thirty to check on him, okay?"

"Okay. What's your name sir?"

He was signing the charge slip. "Charles Donaldson."

He opened the door and was about bowled over by a young man charging in. "Where's the stupid dog. I'll take him home."

"Sir, you'll be charged with animal abuse."

"It's my damn dog!"

"Someone is willing to take responsibility for the dog. You just need to sign a release of ownership so you can't reclaim it if it lives."

"Where do I sign?"

Charles was standing at the door watching and listening. His sad face was transforming into anger and I was afraid we were going to need to call the police because of a brawl. But the young man stormed back out and Charles let him go. After a moment, he too, finally left. I hoped he wouldn't run the fella over with the salt truck.

The surgery went well. We got the internal bleeding stopped, set both broken hind legs, removed a ruptured eyeball, packed the socket and pulled the skin over the packing.

After it had healed a bit and we were sure of no infection, we would pull the packing out and sew the skin permanently over the empty socket.

When we came out Sue was gone for the evening. Margot was cleaning the exam rooms. Conner had his feet up on the counter.

"What are you still doing here?" asked Clint. "You've already put in a long day."

"Had to make sure you got this." He picked up a wad of bills and spread them like a hand of cards. "Here's another fifty towards the dog's care. Everyone in the waiting room donated. Charles came by at five thirty to check on the dog. Said he'd call in the morning."

"Let's hope the dog lives to thank them," I said. "I'm going to stay a few hours to keep an eye on him."

"Madison, go home. I'll come down every couple hours to check on him."

"I'll go about nine o'clock. You can take over from there. So go relax a bit."

Conner and Margot left. Clint wasn't gone long. He brought a meat loaf sandwich and a cup of steaming vegetable soup. He had brought his as well and pulled up a chair. We blew gently on our soup to cool it and munched on our sandwiches in companionable silence for awhile. I got up to peek at the dog and when I came back I broached the subject weighing on my mind.

"Clint, have you developed your saddle club plans any further?"

"Sure have. John already has seven youngsters he wants to target for members. He's chatting them up to see if they have the interest it would take."

"You want this to be a free program, don't you?"

"Monetarily so, but they will have care responsibilities, grade point averages to maintain, and I hope eventually community service requirements. I know you're wondering how we're going to finance, right?"

I nodded.

"Except for the stables which are yours, and you can kick us out at anytime, I'll be footing the whole thing. I have several horses purchased, waiting for their new home to be finished. I even have an order of feed, hay and straw ready to be shipped."

"But how...?"

"Having had no wife to spend all my money, I've invested and made good. I'm pretty wealthy."

I smiled at him. "That's great."

"No, Madison, you're great. I don't think you realize what you've done to this town...for this clinic. I was ready to retired and take up fly fishing but you've instilled a new interest, intensity, and enthusiasm in my life. Business has doubled. Even more than that, you've shown people that it feels good to be generous. Just look at that fifty dollars in pocket change to help this dog. They didn't have to do that."

"I'm sure it was more because Charles was generous."

"Partly yes. But word has gotten around about Cindy riding for free at Phoenix, the people you've hired as employees, the help you're giving to Arielle, lessons for Darla, and the McMullens have something to donate their time to now. If people responded to Charles' generosity, it's because you've set the example of believing in people.

"Let me tell you about Charles. He's a recovering alcoholic. Once upon a time he was a wealthy lawyer. He took on a wealthy doctor as a client. The doctor was accused of running down a child under the influence of a bit of liquor. Charles turned it into a noble thing that the doctor was rushing to the hospital to help with an emergency surgery...denied the amount of alcohol...blamed the parents for not knowing where their twelve year old daughter was at nine P.M. on a school night. Charles' own daughter was twelve at the time.

"Charles was already drinking by then but it got heavy soon after that. His wife divorced him and left with their daughter for the west coast. He lost everything. He was sleeping in his car. One winter a big brown dog came along and Charles let the dog in the car with him. Their combined body warmth probably kept them both from freezing to death. That seemed to give Charles the will to get sober. He got a job to get dog food instead of liquor. The longer he's been sober the better jobs he can get.

"At first people were critically watching whether he would remain sober or not. Now they're making efforts to help him. He has taken in quite a number of stray dogs. He lives west of town in a run down place with all these strays. He just got the city job and let me tell you...it was because of your example that they voted to give him a chance."

"Does he have help supporting all those strays?"

"Nope. Does it all on his own paycheck, however small it's been. I heard there were times he went without eating, and heat in his ramshackle place to be able to feed the dogs."

"What a story."

"Most people have a story."

I set down the soup I had ignored during the telling and went in to check on the dog.

"Has he had any severe stress episodes that could cause him to start drinking again?" I asked when I returned.

"I can't think of any. Why?"

"The dog is dead."

Chapter 19

Arielle was working with Darla on Roxy when I went to the stables on Wednesday evening. "How's it going, ladies?"

Darla brought Roxy to a smooth halt in front of me and gave her enough rein to stretch her neck. Arielle answered first.

"Darla is doing great, Madison, and Mom and Dad said it was okay to bring Cherry here as long as I'm responsible for paying the boarding fee."

"It's a gift, Arielle. Anyway you are more than paying for it."

"It's so fun and easy. I don't feel like I'm doing much."

"I'll have Martin go out to get her tomorrow morning. Is that okay?"

"Can he come before I leave for school?"

"No problem. How are the grades?"

"Still at the top."

"Want to teach a couple more lessons?"

"Oh, yes." Her dark eyes sparkled."

"We have a few junior high girls that want a group lesson. You'll need to teach them how to groom and tack up. They're all friends paying for the lessons out of their allowances. It might be a challenge to keep them serious enough not to get hurt. You'll have to pair them up with a horse best suited to their personalities and abilities. You've been riding them all so you should know the horses pretty well. Think you can do it?"

"Do I get to use Roxy and Zip to assess the girls?"

"Yes, you do."

"I'm sure I can do it."

"Good girl. Oh, and if it's too much, you must tell me Arielle...I know I'm putting a lot on you. Remember, the grades are of paramount importance."

"I promise to tell you if it's too much."

I turned to Darla. "And how are you doing?"

"I love it here Madison. I feel good about my progress but you'll have to ask Arielle how I'm really doing."

I turned back to Arielle. "your prognosis, instructor?"

"She's willing to work, does a good job on the chores, she handles criticism well, she works hard at her riding skills and is improving rapidly."

I turned back to Darla. "Darla that is a truly professional report. Shelly and Ashley have been watching and basically that's what they've said as well. I'm real proud of you. Are you interested in showing?"

Her face went slack. "No, not really. I just want to enjoy horses."

"Okay. Keep in mind that you can use equestrian events as a scholarship into some colleges." I saw a spark light in her eyes. "Let us know if you change your mind."

"Can I keep taking lessons?"

"As long as you're willing to do the chores to earn them. Showing was not a mandate."

She sighed and smiled. "Thank you so much Madison. Arielle said I'm ready to move to Argo."

"That's great. We need Roxy, Deek and Zip for those beginners coming in."

I had taken the week between Christmas and New Year's off. I was working Parcheesie twice a day over the stadium jumps. After a springtime refresher over cross country, I felt he'd be ready for his debut as an eventer. If Lori was ready, I'd pass him off to her. I had smiled when Lori actually commented to me one day, she thought Parcheesie was the ultimate and hoped to own a horse like him some day.

I had answered, "Keep improving your equestrian skills so you're prepared when the opportunity presents itself."

"Do you think it really will?"

"I have no doubt"

I had put him through the upper level dressage test and he did great. I felt a satisfaction in realizing he just needed a break from it and introduced to other challenges.

I had more time to watch Lori's progress and was sure she would be able to handle Parcheesie when the Spring show circuit would begin. I was sure she would rise through the ranks quickly.

I was watching Arielle ride the other horses and noted her progress in jumping on Casablanca Knight. She would need a new mount soon.

I made it a point to sit in on lessons as well and asked students at every level what they thought of the horses and instructors. I liked what I heard.

Cherry Tart arrived Thursday morning. Arielle was there after school to ride and started her over poles.

I was relaxing with a book Thursday afternoon when Jake called.

"I've found a great jumper for advanced students. He's a Swedish Warmblood, Jumping Jack Flash."

"Great. Have you already checked him out?"

"Yep. We can pick him up anytime."

"That's our last stall. I promised John a stall if he should find a horse before the saddle club stables are complete.'

"How close are they?"

"The stalls are up. They're putting in the wash bay and grooming area. Saddle racks need installed in the tack room."

"What are the chances he'll find that special horse in the next couple days."

"You're right. Did you pay for Flash already?"

"Yep. Send Martin for him. Here's the address and phone number."

I called Phil McMullen to let him know we'd be bringing a new horse for quarantine. Martin and I left immediately in the Phoenix truck pulling our yellow and orange two-horse trailer.

It took two and a half hours to get to Charles Town, load Flash who was a perfect gentleman, trailer him to the McMullen pasture and get home. I no sooner picked up my book as it was growing dark outside, when the phone rang.

"Madison, this is John Smith."

My heart skipped.

"You won't believe the horse I've found. A full sister to Zip Lock and Spiffy Zip. Her name is Zip Zip Zeebang. Clint has already done a vet check. Is that stall still available?"

"No."

There was shocked silence.

"Don't worry. Go ahead and purchase her if you really want her. She has to go to quarantine first anyway. Do you need help with transporting her?"

"Yes."

"Where is she?"

"Drummond."

"When do you want to go get her?"

"Actually this is my day off."

"Okay. Come on out here and ride with Jeff to go get her. Take her out to McMullen's place. Hopefully, by the time both horses are out of quarantine the stables will be done."

"Both horses?"

"Yeah. We just brought home another jumper."

"Are you sure?"

"The stables are done. The amenities just need completed. It'll be fine John."

But it wasn't. Flash laid his ears flat against his head and charged the paddock fence. Zippy retreated to the far side of her own fenced area. Phil called and explained the situation.

"He won't even let me in the paddock with him to clean up the piles or groom him."

What had happened, I wondered? That didn't sound like the horse I had helped load and bring home. It was already dark. I'd go out in the morning.

It took only a moment to see that Flash was really not liking his situation. I asked Phil when it started.

"When he first got here, he looked around and then moped as if he wasn't pleased. When I went out to groom him, he acted a bit testy. He exploded when they brought the mare in. Good thing you put up the double fenced individual paddocks."

I had two days until my wedding. I was feeling a bit nervous. I just wanted to relax to calm myself. Or was it better to be busy so I wouldn't think about it? I wasn't sure but it didn't seem to make a difference. I had to deal with this.

Jake was totally shocked when I told him of Flash's attitude. "He wasn't like that when I went to see him. I rode him and watched someone else ride him."

"Was he drugged?"

"No. I checked his eyes and gums. He was alert."

"I'm going to ask for Cindy's assistance."

Mrs. Ley was hesitant at first until I assured her Cindy wouldn't have to get close to the horse if it showed signs of aggression. "I certainly wouldn't want to jeopardize her safety," I assured her.

They came earlier than her riding time. Jake and I drove them to Phil's. Zippy was inside her stall, afraid to come out. Phil and Betty came out to watch. Flash was close to the gate.

As our car pulled in, his head shot up but as we piled out it dropped morosely again.

Cindy started confidently toward the gate with a smile on her face. Mrs. Ley grabbed her hand to hold her back. Flash laid his ears back, turned away and even threw a kick that hit the rail with a resounding crack. Cindy paused and then started crying.

I knelt beside Cindy, my knee in slush, soaking up a cold that went all the way to my heart. "What's wrong with Flash, Cindy?"

Cindy hugged her mother to bury her face in the wool winter coat Mrs. Ley was wearing and cried louder.

"That's enough. Let's go. Gloria, I'm sorry. I didn't know it would distress her so."

We clambered back into the car. I told Phil not to endanger himself while trying to care for him.

"Jake, maybe we should call his previous owners and get his history."

"Good idea. I did bring the video of him in a few shows."

Cindy was still whimpering and didn't want to ride. Jake convinced her to at least say "Hi" to Zip and Deek or they'd think she was mad at them. I felt horrible about ruining her evening at the stables. Mrs. Ley had once told me it was the high light of Cindy's week.

The week between Christmas and New Years was always light on visitors. Even some students took a break along with several boarders who were caught up in the holiday mania. Saturday night was New Year's Eve. In just a little over thirty hours I would officially be Mrs. Andrews.

"Jake, I really feel unsettled. Can you fill Shelly in on what happened? I just want to go soak in a hot tub."

He looked concerned. "Not getting cold feet are you?"

I looped my arm through his. "No way. I can hardly wait to finally be your wife."

"Here, take the video; watch it. It will reassure you. I'll call the seller from Shelly's office. If I get any kind of answer I'll give you a buzz. Have the phone close."

Angie had chicken a la king made. I could never understand how she knew how to have it available and hot just when I was ready. As I ate, I told her I'd see her Monday and that she should not party too hearty. She left in a drizzle. It was suppose to turn to freezing rain.

I was soaking, relaxing, almost asleep despite the water cooling, when the phone rang. It jolted me awake and made my heart race.

"Jake?" I asked shakily.

"It's me. All they said was the evidence is on the video and if the horse has a problem, we caused it. They said the sale is final. That makes me think something is being hidden. Do you want to take him back?"

"No. You've never been wrong about a horse, Jake. Something happened between that place and here that he wasn't expecting. Maybe he misses someone. Cindy's reaction tells me the horse is hurting emotionally. I think we'll get an answer. It'll just take time. If I recall, you were quite taken by him. He'll be worth the effort."

"Alright. Are you still in the tub?"

I could hear a smile in his voice. "Are you leering?"

"It won't be long Mrs. Andrews."

"I love when you talk domestic to me."

I got out of the tub, wrapped in a long terry robe and put the video in the VCR. I sat spell bound as Flash made clean rounds over five and six foot fences, oxers and in and outs time after time. Right in the middle of the sequences was a close up of Flash and a very pretty young woman; their faces side by side. That was a clue, I was sure. We needed to know who that was.

The phone rang. "Jake?"

"No, this is Gloria Ley."

"Oh, Gloria. I'm glad you called. How is Cindy?"

"That's why I called, Madison. A lot of times, if she's upset about something, she'll work it out in play. When we got home she went to her Barbie and Barbie's horse."

"And?"

"The horse jumped the fence. Barbie fell off. Someone put a white sheet over Barbie and took her away. The horse waits for Barbie to come back. The horse goes to another place and wonders if Barbie doesn't love him anymore; if it was his fault she went away."

I felt tears running down my face. "Poor Flash. He must have loved that young woman very much."

"What young woman?"

"In the middle of the video Jake brought, there's a head shot of Flash and the young woman who rode him."

"Now what?"

"I don't know. We need to help him understand she isn't coming back and it wasn't his fault. It's up to him to decide if he'll move on."

"What if it was his fault? Maybe he balked at a fence."

"After seeing him take the fences on the video, I can't picture that. Did Cindy show him balking?"

"No."

"Thanks for letting me know, Gloria, and again I'm sorry that it upset Cindy."

I wrapped myself in a blanket and watched rain trickle down the bedroom window until it turned to ice and hit the panes with tiny pings.

Chapter 20

I awoke to a huge moon hanging just above the tops of the pine trees in the back yard. Their greenery draped in ice drooped beneath burdens too great to bear. The deep snow shown silver with a frosting of ice.

The hot soak in the tub had really relaxed me. I felt rested but a bit stiff from having fallen asleep in the chair. I stretched, trying to work out the kinks, and went to the kitchen to make a cup of tea. I changed into flannel pajamas and crawled between the sheets. This will be my last day as a single woman, I thought, and fell asleep leaving the tea to cool untouched on the bedside table.

I heard the door bell ring several times before managing to surface from a deep sleep. I bounded down the stairs and flung open the door. A burst of freezing wind and Melissa holding her hood closed at the neck burst in the door pulling her two-wheeled dolly hauling a trunk-like container. I closed the door against the hoar.

"Good morning."

"Brrr. What a cold snap."

"Let me get you something to warm you up. Tea, coffee, hot chocolate?"

"Coffee; one sugar please. I brought my own Irish Crème flavoring.

"Where's Chelsea?"

"With an elderly neighbor lady working as a companion for the day."

"That's nice. Gives you a baby sitter while she thinks she's doing the babysitting and getting paid for it."

"I'm not sure she doesn't see through the ruse, but she likes having her own money so she goes along with it."

"As long as it works. Anything I can do to help you?"

"Not in those PJs. If you get dressed I'll let you help me bring in the rest of my stuff. Then you're outta here."

I was proud of Mr. Ballard. He had built the stables knowing what winter could do. All the water faucets were working fine. In the new stable, however, there were already frozen pipes. I called the company doing the work.

"Not enough insulation," he explained.

"Whatever the reason, I expect the problem to be taken care of...yes?"

"This is new years eve day."

"The insulation should have been adequate before you started putting up the stalls. There are purchased horses waiting for those stalls."

"That's what you told me. I thought you wanted those stalls up so you could get the horses in."

"Not by skimping on foundation work."

"We'll be back on the job January 2."

It was a serious setback. I was upset that I hadn't supervised closer. We could stable horses but would have to haul water from the main stables. I wasn't eager to do that.

The pastures had a foot of frozen snow covering them. The horses could get cut on the sharp crust so we turned them in the arena, a few compatible equines at a time to let them kick up their heels and stretch out the kinks. I didn't think anyone would show up to ride in these temperatures. I helped muck stalls, scrub water buckets and feed pans, and gave most of the stable hands the rest of the day off. A few remained in case someone did show up. They'd stay in the heated break room. Shelly brought out some games and a jigsaw puzzle. The window faced the drive and parking lot. They'd be available if anyone came.

I returned to the house about noon wanting another hot soak, hoping it would relax me into a nap. I wanted to be able to stay awake well past midnight. Wonderful food aromas filled the main floor of the house.

I had just gingerly gotten into the tub, breathing short gasps as my legs and arms turned red, when the phone rang. I dried one hand and was grateful I hadn't moved the phone when I expected Jake's call the previous day.

"Hello?"

"Madison, this is Jake."

"You aren't calling it off are you?"

He laughed. "No way. I'll be there but my mind will be on other things tonight. I wanted to tell you, when I took Cindy back to say hello to Zip and Deek yesterday, Arielle was working Cherry Tart over poles. Cindy stopped to watch and then said, 'Cherry won't jump. She thinks it's unladylike.'"

I laughed. I guess that's the end of that, then."

"Maybe Arielle can get another horse for three-day eventing and use Cherry to give dressage lessons."

"That's an idea, but Arielle is going to be disappointed."

"Well, not every horse is an eventer."

"That's true."

"See you this evening, my love."

"Promise?"

"Promise."

It was a two hour nap. I put on sweat pants and a floppy sweater. I paused to gaze at the white gown and black tux hanging in the closet. I reached into the pocket of the tuxedo jacket and pulled out the matching rings. In less than nine hours.... I put them back and went down to the kitchen where Melissa had her hands around another mug of Irish crème coffee.

"How's it going?"

"Fine. Everything is ready for the final step. I was just ready to go grab a nap."

"I'm going to make myself a sandwich. Want one?"

"No, thanks."

"Okay. Enjoy your nap. A hot soak will relax you."

"Oh, that sounds heavenly."

"Towels and robes are in the hall cupboard. Help yourself."

"Thanks."

I called down to the break room in the stable. "Everything okay down there?"

"Yep," Shelly answered. "I'm about ready to call it quits. Josh, Carl, and Brock came in to feed and lock up shop."

"You must be exhausted. Will you be able to make it to midnight?'

"I'll make it. Don't worry. Nine o'clock, right?'

I made a fire in the hearth and looked for a book to curl up with. I paced. I went up and looked at our gown and tux again. I paced and took out my gown to hold the beaded satin next to my skin. Then, afraid I was jinxing myself, I hung it up, got another cup of tea and went back to the fire and book.

I finally heard Melissa come down the stairs and looked at the clock. Finally I could get ready. I wore a silky maroon shift with spaghetti straps, and a string of tiny pearls with matching ear rings. It would be easy to get out of and into my gown at the right moment. The jewelry matched the beads on my wedding gown.

Jake was bringing my bouquet and his boutonniere with him. The mini-frig in my bedroom would keep them fresh until they were needed. I was wondering where Jake was. He should be here by now to help greet the guests.

How would he get the flowers up to the bedroom without attracting attention if there were guests here already? I felt queasy in my stomach. How was I going to make it another three to four hours without giving away the secret?

The doorbell rang as I was descending the stairs. It was Marshall.

"Whew, you look gorgeous."

"Thanks, Marshall."

"I want to get pictures of your guests while they're sober."

"It's a dry party," I said looking around him. "Have you seen Jake?"

"No. I talked to him yesterday."

"He should be here by now."

"Wasn't he to pick up the flowers before coming?"

"He was supposed to get them by noon. The flower shop was closing early."

"That's probably the problem. He forgot and is frantically trying to find a suitable bouquet to take its place."

"Oh, don't say that," I groaned.

"If that's the worst that goes wrong, you'll be doing well, Madison."

"What could be worse at a wedding?"

"No guests showing up. The roads are still icy. Or the preacher forgetting."

"Okay, okay. I'll take any flowers he can find," I laughed.

"I'm going to stash rolls of film all over the place so I can reload no matter where I'm at without making a fuss, okay?"

"That's fine. Sounds like you really thought out the situation."

The door bell rang regularly. Melissa circulated with hors devours and some fantastic non-alcoholic drinks. Clint, the

Rusnecks, Jake's family trickled in. I opened the door once and saw Conner in the glow of the outside light going up the steps to Shelly's apartment and they were the next guests through my door.

Russ and Brandi hadn't seen or talked to Jake either. "Maybe he's planning a practical joke," offered Russ.

My heart skipped a beat. He had no way of knowing of the planned wedding; no way of knowing the effect his words had on me. I went into my office and dialed Jake's cell phone number. I got no signal. I dialed his office phone. His voice on the answering machine steadied me.

"Jake, where are you sweetie? Please don't play games. It's ten thirty. You should be here by now."

I called his home phone and left the same message.

The doorbell rang again. I went out into the foyer. Melissa had answered the door and John Smith stood inside, hat in hand. I had to laugh.

"The neighbors complained already? We're just getting revved up."

"Madison," John wasn't smiling. "Jake's been in a serious accident."

My knees felt weak. "Is he all right?"

"Let me take you to the hospital."

"How bad is it?"

"Get your coat, Madison."

Blackness was crowding my eyesight. I felt hands grasping my arms even as I felt like I was falling and my stomach rejected remnants of the sandwich I had eaten at noon.

Chapter 21

How long had it been? Days and days of no shower, no food, pitying faces coming and going, wandering about the house that Jake had found for me, in which he should be living with me. I shuffled in soiled flannel pajamas and slippers from room to room, occasionally finding a roll of film in some hiding place where Marshall had stashed it for easy access. I would remember, cry, and scream "You promised you'd be here! You promised!"

Angie came everyday to set food in front of me; clean up what I hadn't eaten the day before. She chatted about the weather, her boyfriend watching sports all the time, about everyone missing me. I was glad when she left in the evening.

I sat in the chair and watched as the ice melted drip by drip, and the pines bent beneath burdens of snow finally stood tall again. I needed to stand tall again. I needed to get back to work. I needed to come back to life. But what life would there be without the man who had awakened me to love and the brightness of the days in the wake of that love? I finally took a shower, put on jeans and marveled at how loose they were. I had to use a belt to keep them snug about my shrunken waist.

The late afternoon sun glared off the snow and when I stepped inside the stable, I had to pause a moment for my eyes to adjust. My favorite earthy smells wafted to my nostrils and I couldn't help leaning back against the door, inhaling deeply and listening to the clip clop of a horse being led down the aisle to the grooming bays. I took another deep breath but had to move as I felt someone pushing on the door to get in. Shelly folded me into her arms.

"It's so good to see you out at last."

"I thought I'd better tend to business." I gave her a weak smile.

"We've been tending it for you, Madison. We've followed through on everything you set in motion before...before New Year's Day."

I closed my eyes and felt myself sway. Shelly put her arm through mine and pulled me forward into the stables warmed by equine bodies and the chatter of stable hands. They fell silent when they saw me and then offered timid greetings.

"Hey there, Madison."

"Good to see you."

"We've missed you."

I smiled at them. There had been no slacking. The stables were spic and span; no accumulated dirt, no cobwebs in corners; no crusty water buckets or feed pans.

Shelly guided me into our wing. I stopped to pet each of our horses. They all came to their stall guards to greet me. Argo and Parcheesie whickered. I stroked them and couldn't help feel the muscles in Parcheesie's neck. I unsnapped his stall guard and went in. Shelly restrained him by a hand on his forehead as I ran my hand down a firm back and taut haunches.

"Wow, is he fit!"

"Arielle, Lori and I have all been riding him. I give him regular messages to keep him supple. I think you should show him this season."

"No, I want Lori on him."

"Lori is doing great over four footers but she isn't quite ready for Parcheesie. I've been taking him over five footers and it's hardly taxing him. But we have to remember he is still new to jumping. A couple more months, maybe, and they'll be ready for each other."

"Then maybe you should show him this first year."

"I'm just a barn manager."

"Shelly, you are one awesome barn manager but you are much more than that. Besides being the best friend a body could have, you're an exceptional horsewoman. I've seen you ride. Get Parcheesie ready for Lori and I'll be sure to get you a horse of your own to show."

"Madison, I really like riding all the horses, getting to know them, helping match them up with incoming and progressing students. I don't need one of my own."

"You are so like Jake in that way." I heard my voice crack. "Then will you show one of ours to represent Phoenix stable?"

She smiled. "THAT, I would love to do."

"How's his dressage. Is he showing resistance?"

"No. Arielle has been working in that and has fine tuned him. They're improving each other. That girl is one awesome trainer. She knows how to bring out the best in a horse. She's having a hard time with Cherry Tart, though. Cherry did okay over poles and six inchers that she could step over but refuses to actually jump. Arielle came off the first couple times Cherry stopped and tried to shy away."

I chuckled but my heart constricted when I said, "The last time I talked to Jake he let me know Cindy said Cherry won't jump. She thinks it's unladylike."

Shelly laughed. "We'd better let Arielle know. She's going to be disappointed. She loves jumping."

We moved on and no horse was at the door that was closed. Flash stood at the back, his head hung low. He had lost weight. I leaned against the stall bars and closed my eyes. Now I could empathize with his loss. Behind my closed eyelids I saw the young blond woman that had been Flash's owner and rider taken away beneath the white sheet. And then I saw Jake and the sheet pulled up over his face. I saw the two of them hold hands and walk away. A sob escaped my throat.

I felt a whuffle of warm breath on my face. I looked up to see Flash blurred through my tears, pushing his nose against the bars. I slid the door back, stepped into the stall and wrapped my arms around his neck. He wrapped his head around my body in a hug of his own.

Shelly quietly backed away.

Each morning I got up, I looked out the windows or down the road my car traveled to the clinic and noticed the days were getting longer; getting light earlier. I was looking for the brightness that Jake's love had brought into my life but the colors weren't as vivid. The ache inside was a constant companion which seemed to dull everything around me.

Conner seemed particularly attentive. He brought me strawberries dipped in chocolate or yogurt sprinkled with granola for lunch on the days we worked together. It concerned me. I thought he and Shelly were an item. I wanted them to connect. I thought they were a perfect couple; she deserved a significant other and no one could take Jake's place for me.

One day he finally made it clear where our relationship stood.

"Do you believe in things happening for a reason, Madison?"

A lump formed in my throat that I couldn't swallow. Tears pooled in my eyes. I couldn't answer. I could not believe there was a reason for Jake dying.

"I was drowning in sorrow, just as you are, when I sent my resume to this clinic. You see, last New Year's Eve my wife and daughter were killed by a drunk driver, just as Jake was. I thought I'd never want to live again. I had to get away from... there.

"I've not been here but a few months but I realize I was guided here. I've met Shelly; she makes me want to live again. And there's you who has lost the love of your life and needs encouragement to live again. I can give you that because I've been there. You don't think you'll ever want to let go of Jake and the memories, but you will get through this Madison. You will."

The tears streamed down my cheeks. I knew what he said was true...but not yet. All I could do was nod and walk away.

Chapter 22

I turned Parcheesie over to Shelly and started working with Flash. First I just groomed and lunged him. Then one day Taylor was taking some jumps on Casablanca Knight and Flash got excited. His ears pricked on head held high. He blew and pranced as he watched CK take the jumps. I had the feeling Flash was ready to let go of his pain and live again.

Being a Swedish Warmblood, Flash was the largest horse we had on the place. It took awhile to find a saddle with a good fit.

My first time on his back, I was shaking with excitement. He shook his head and pranced. I could only ask him to give me certain gaits but he was a gentleman and gave what I requested. As a reward, I took him over a few four footers. Shelly was working Parcheesie at the same time. The sound of pounding hoof beats hardly muffled in the arena sand sent my blood rushing and suddenly we too were flying over the five footers. As excited as I was, I was still paying attention and could tell Flash had a lot more to give. It was time to get serious.

I could hardly wait these days to get into the arena with Flash. He would whinny when he saw me. I think if he could, he would have saddled himself.

I had noticed for some time, the van that had Montaine Saddle Club on the side and its weekend cargo of young boys. The boys never strayed beyond the new stable and arena area. I decided it was time to pay a visit.

All six boys were mounted as I walked in. All six dismounted. Clint took me to each one to introduce us to each other. They ranged in age from seven to seventeen. Each shook my hand and called me ma'am.

I asked each boy the name of his horse and what he liked best about the horse and the saddle club. The youngest boy, Kyle, had a pinto named Taco Pal. The young fella showed no fear on his pale face of the big animal he held by the reins. His eyes were direct and wizened.

I looked them over and could only imagine what their lives had been to create the anger, hopelessness, desperation in the eyes before me. Some held onto the reins defiantly daring me to take this good thing from them. Others held loosely expecting it to be taken away. I was glad Clint wanted to start this program. It was only seven boys in a sea of thousands, but maybe these seven would be better for having had the experience.

Arielle had accepted the fact that Cherry Tart didn't want to jump. To her credit, she didn't let her disappointment keep her from working the mare in dressage.

I was watching closely the progress of Lori and Arielle as they took the jumps on Casablanca Knight. They both looked ready to move on. Because Parcheesie was new to jumping, although he was doing great, I wanted Shelly to keep working him. Flash knew what he was doing. I wanted to see if the girls could handle him.

Both Arielle and Lori were excited about riding Flash. They started over two and three footers. I rode him over the five footers twice a week. Lori could only come once a week. Arielle filled in the other four days improving her skill rapidly. We started raising the bars for her. Flash handled it all with ease.

The three girl friends were still taking lessons together but were faltering in their enthusiasm. They hadn't realized it was so much work. I listened in one Wednesday evening as Arielle explained the benefits of firm thighs, good posture, confidence and poise.

"But it's boring," moaned Alecia.

"You'll all get more exciting mounts when I'm sure you can handle them without hurting them. When you ride, you're responsible for protecting your mount from harm or abuse. If you ride into situations where he gets hurt often enough, he'll quit trusting you."

"What about us," wailed Jennifer.

"If you protect him, when the time comes, your mount will do the same for you."

"We're in a big box," scoffed Courtney looking around the arena. "How can we hurt them?"

"By pulling on their mouth, sitting out of balance, bouncing in the saddle when riding or mounting. These three horses are really tolerant but other horses won't be."

With some satisfaction I saw all three girls try to straighten up without appearing to do so.

Chapter 23

The snow began to diminish, boarders came more often, Taylor got his driver's license and asked for a job. We assigned him to the saddle club barn. He brought Lori along so she could ride Flash more often. Taylor worked and then took Arielle home. They were showing signs of being a couple.

Gloria Miller and another boarder, Glen Thorn, were riding together a lot. Even Cindy found herself a beau by wandering into the saddle club area. Kyle found her. She told him Taco Pal really liked him.

"How do you know?" asked Kyle.

"He told me."

Kyle didn't doubt her. He put her astride Taco Pal bare back and led the horse and its passenger back to the main stable area where Mrs. Ley was searching for her.

Joe had taken over Jake's position as Cindy's riding guardian. He was turning into a great horseman. We were watching him closely and starting to search for a suitable mount that he could show for Phoenix.

I soon discovered that Flash's welcoming whinny was sometimes tinged with impatience and he welcomed whoever was coming toward his stall. It wasn't us he loved. It was the jumping. He didn't like the control of dressage. He would never be a good three day eventer. Show jumping and cross country would be his forte. I let Joe take over my riding slot on Flash and I backed off a bit so I'd have time to search for his special mount.

I could barely get through the days now that I wasn't on a super horse regularly. Now that Joe took my place on Flash, I filled my time with work at the clinic, surfing the net for a new mount for Joe, looking over the show schedules, conferring with Shelly on which shows we'd attend and riding whichever horse needed a bit of exercise. I had to muse once again how I once thought that I would have been happy with a backyard horse and how it just wasn't true. I craved the energy, excitement and enthusiasm of a horse that reveled in his athleticism.

More frequently I was catching myself staring out the window into my personal forest of pines, lost in time. My mind seemed to be searching for my heart which was languishing after...what, who? I almost couldn't remember.

Jake's masculine scent was the first thing to elude my efforts to make his memory whole. Then evaporated the memory of his touch, the sound of his voice, the color of his eyes and then the smile he was so rarely without. At the last when I thought of him he was only a retreating back holding hands with the young woman who no longer rode Flash.

I cried myself to sleep the first time I realized I hadn't thought of Jake in over two days. I felt I was losing him all over again because the remembering was diminishing. It was as if my tears helped to wash him out of my mind. I awoke and continued to live without him; without thinking of him for days. Something would remind me and I would cry again for the emptiness he had left within me and for the lengthening time between thoughts of him until he was just the sound on someone's lips to which I no longer reacted. Finally the crying stopped. I lived and moved and had my being at the clinic and on any Phoenix horse that needed me at any given moment.

The show season was about to begin. Everyone was working hard. The snow and ice had disappeared. For a day we had a view of green grass and brown mud and then overnight big heavy flakes piled up six inches of white again. The pines hung heavy with the new burden God gave them to carry. I felt the same heaviness. The sun melted it all with its forgiving rays the next day and the pines stood upright encouraging me to do the same.

Marshall invited me to meet him for lunch one day at Grandma's Diner before my eleven o'clock shift at the clinic. I saw Charles Donaldson sitting alone and went to his booth to say hello. I apologized for not saving the dog.

"Wasn't your fault," he answered.

"How are you doing?"

"Fine."

"I heard you've taken in a couple strays."

"They seem to come looking for me."

I smiled. "I can understand why. You're a very compassionate man. If any need spayed or neutered, I'll donate the service."

He looked up in surprise.

"And I'll give first shots at cost."

"That's awfully nice of you."

"Why don't you start an animal rescue?"

"Not sure I could swing it financially."

"Well, I'll help in any way I can."

"Thank you."

I saw Marshall walk in. "You take care, okay?"

"I will."

I moved toward the table Marshall had chosen.

"Good morning," he greeted.

I smiled. "Morning. I brought you something. I opened my backpack and pulled out a brown lunch bag with the collected rolls of film.

He smiled. "Thanks."

"How's business?"

"Great. People selling and buying houses all over the place."

"I guess I was thinking of the photography."

"Oh. Well, I've got a good bit of that business also."

"Is that your passion?"

The waitress arrived to take our orders.

"You know Madison, I'm a lot like you. I really love both my jobs. I get immense satisfaction helping people find their dream homes, and taking a good photo. Could you pick between Phoenix and the clinic if you had to let one of them go?"

"Ah, I know what you mean. I think Phoenix would win out over the clinic, but yes, I love both."

"Do you have time for anything else?"

"My time is mine to control. I still have a good bit of flexibility thanks to great co-workers at both places. Clint is hiring Vicki Torrence. So that will free up even more time."

Marshall's club sandwich and my salad arrived.

"Have you seen the previews of The White Balloon? It's a Carnes film festival award winner."

"No. Does it look good?"

"Yes. I was wondering if you'd like to go see it? We could get something to eat beforehand at Clancy's."

"Sounds good." I stuffed lettuce drenched in Italian dressing into my mouth, kept my eyes on the tomato waiting its turn and fought the guilt squeezing my heart.

As though sensing my discomfort, Marshall changed the subject. "How's the saddle club working out?"

"I think those boys are really enjoying themselves. A few are having a hard time with grades and Clint has a hard time enforcing the GPA requirement. Some of them could use some tutoring."

"Why don't you post the need at the stables?"

"That's an idea. It would get more people involved which could only be a positive factor in those lives. Do you want to take one on?"

"You know, I just might. Maybe introduce the fella to photography."

"Marshall, the one I want you to mentor is Charlie Albright. He's seventeen and will turn eighteen in April. He's been in foster care since he was ten. At the end of the school term he's out on his own. No job, no place to live, grades barely good enough to graduate; definitely not good enough to get into college."

"Wow. That's a pickle to be in."

"He's kind of wild-eyed. Clint says it's because he's really scared. Afraid they'll boot him out of the saddle club also."

"What's Clint going to do?"

"He's going to give him a promotion. He gets to keep riding Charlie, his horse. Shelly is going to try to teach him how to manage the saddle club barn. Plus he'll take over all the work over there. Taylor was doing it but we can use him at the main barns."

"So Charlie rides Charlie."

"Yeah. He said that's why he picked that horse. I'd hate to see him settle for a mucking job unless he really likes horses and does good at managing the barn. But Clint has his doubts. He really likes riding but seems to do only enough work to get by. Maybe you could help him to explore other interests and options."

"Big brother relationship?"

"Something like that. Maybe all we can do is stabilize him until his fear lessens and he can start thinking and making his own plans."

"So for now, he has a job. He still needs a roof and wheels. I'll see what I can do. Shall I come out this weekend to meet him?"

"That would be great."

"And I'll see you Wednesday to go see the film. Six o'clock okay?"

"Yeah," I answered over my shoulder as I made my dash to the clinic. The guilt of dating Marshall four months after Jake's death knotted my stomach. "You left me, Jake!" I protested. "Don't you dare talk to me about loyalty."

Chapter 24

The ground was thawing and the spring rains began. Days alternated from previews of summer to reminders of winter. Russ and Brandi got married and left for Hawaii. I cried throughout the ceremony, but tried to smile as they kissed me good-bye. Brandi gave me a long hug that endangered my composure. My mantra had become 'Life goes on'. Indeed the activity of life was all around. Only my heart didn't remember.

Mrs. Ley had invited Kyle for family outings. His single Mom, who sometimes was invited as well, was grateful. Marshall and Charlie had hit it off pretty good. Taylor struck up a friendship with Wade who rode an appaloosa named Chief Joseph. Taylor used Deek or George to trail ride with Wade. They even extended their friendship outside the stable area by going to movies, and an occasional party as well as worked on bringing up Wade's GPA.

Arielle still got a ride home but they now seemed more friends than a couple. Conner took Caden and Little Brown Jug under his tutelage. John started tutoring Brandon on Petey. Tim, on a pinto named Chico, seemed to be doing fine.

Despite having an absentee father and since starting in the saddle club he had attained a high GPA, and became a swimmer for his school. As his community service, he took ten year old Dick on Kanga as his tutorial. The individual attention to the boys soon resulted in higher grades and more smiles. They relaxed and became friendlier.

We came back from our first show with several ribbons and high hopes for the season. The high caliber of our horses drew attention to Phoenix stables and Shelly found a lot of her time was spent returning phone message on her machine. The saddle club attended their first show and although they brought home no first place ribbons, everyone saw the potential and Clint's phone was packed with inquiries from neighboring towns' police departments and schools. He commented he'd like to hire a secretary. We discussed where we could add an office onto the saddle club stables.

Darla came to me tearfully one Wednesday saying she could no longer take lessons or even come to the stables. Her parents were insisting she participate in sports at school with which she could get scholarships, as well as get a job to start saving for college. She was very good in track and swimming. After discussing it with Shelly and Clint, we asked her if she'd like a secretarial job. She could work it around her sports practices and school and could maybe even still ride after her work was done.

Again, I was reminded how fortunate I was that I had the means to have so many horses in my life, and despite my efforts, I could not put that singular joy into everyone's life, no matter how badly they wanted it, or how much they deserved it.

The contractors began work on adding six stalls to each wing of our "T" shaped stable and I eliminated one pasture to add another indoor arena. We hoped to host small shows eventually. The twelve new boarding stalls were already under contract with new boarders.

The saddle club was already planning a "Play Day" event over the July Fourth holiday. They had invited several other equine clubs to participate in barrel racing, pole bending and western pleasure. The Phoenix trail ride was also planned for that weekend. Clint and I had decided the proceeds from both events would go toward establishing a humane society with Charles Donaldson as director and operator.

We told Charles and he cried. "I don't know what to say."

"Say, you love the idea."

He grinned through misty eyes. "I love the idea."

"Start looking for suitable property. Preferably out from town where people won't be disturbed by the barking of dogs, or braying of donkeys."

"You want me to take donkeys?"

"I doubt you'll get much more than dogs and cats," assured Clint. "Wildlife has to go to the Forestry department over in Columbus. They have specially trained caretakers. But if we should find abused equines, you should be ready for them."

"I don't know anything about equines."

"That's where we'll step in to lend a hand."

At our second show, we found a trail to a horse for Joe. Someone said; someone said; here's a phone number. We went to look at him. Boudoir was a Hanovarian. He reminded me of Fritz and I felt a twinge of nostalgia. I rode him. His dressage was impeccable; his jumps well timed and fluid. Joe's eyes glowed but he was hesitant as his own dressage skills were less than perfect.

"He'll make up for your faults until you improve," I encouraged him. I felt the horse was worth the price. He would be an incredible addition to our line of performance horses. We took him home with us to further enhance the reputation of Phoenix stables.

I'd made a habit of sitting in the big overstuffed chair, sipping on a cup of hot tea and going over the plans and results of the day's activities before crawling into bed at night. Tonight was a full moon that played with the back yard forest to create a light and dark striped canvas. I sat watching a couple rabbits nibbling early summer grass.

I was upset tonight. Charlie hadn't like mucking stalls everyday and the math required to calculate the number of bales of hay and pounds of feed to order was beyond him. Marshall had found him a small apartment and loaned him the deposit as well as enough to purchase a beater car. With a month's worth of pay in his pocket, Charlie decided California would be more exciting and warmer in December.

"I'll repay whatever he owes you, Marshall," I offered. "I'm the one that talked you into mentoring him."

"Nonsense. You didn't twist my arm. Loaning him that much money was bad judgment on my part. They aren't all savable. The help came too late. Have you another?"

I admired his willingness to give it another try.

Suddenly, before my eyes the rabbits first froze and then, as a white streak shot from between the big low branched pines, they scattered. The dog snapped one way, but when he missed the rabbit, twisted to chase the other and lost it as well. Then he sat and panted heavily.

I sat shocked at the desperate scene that had just played out before me. The heavy panting made me think that the dog might be hunting because of hunger and not sport. I was stunned even more as I took some slightly warmed left over stew and a bowl of water out to him.

The scrawny body, with lolling tongue and saliva dripping from jowls, clearly wanted to lunge at the food but held back eyeing me. I stepped behind and slid shut the patio doors. I even hid behind the curtains to watch him wolf down the meal, lap up the water and then dash under the nearest evergreen tree.

I stepped out to retrieve the bowls and had to smile and speak to the dirty, white face peering out through the low lying branches. His black eyes watched me intently. Although I softly coaxed, he wouldn't emerge from the protective arms of the tree.

I called Angie before crawling into bed. "Angie, can you pick up some dog food on your way here in the morning?"

"Sure, no problem. Did you get a dog?"

"More like he got me."

In the morning Angie showed up early with the dog food. "Thanks, Angie. I was wondering what I was going to feed him. I didn't want to leave without giving him something."

He came out of hiding to slowly thump his tail against the ground but wouldn't come close.

"Set more out each time he finishes it," I instructed. "When he won't finish the food take it up and don't set any out until four hours later. Give him about a cup of food and give him twenty minutes to eat it. Repeat every four hours."

"Okay. What are you going to name him?"

"I'm not. I'm too busy for a dog. I'll call Charles Donaldson later to see if he'll take him."

About eight o'clock I called Charles and got his answering machine. "I'll pay for shots and to get him healthy," I promised.

I didn't hear from him all day and was beginning to worry that he couldn't take an addition to his already crowded home. He had not yet found suitable land for his rescue facility. I was relieved to see him at Phoenix when I pulled in after work.

"Charles thanks for coming. I hope this means you'll take him even though you don't have your facility yet."

"Actually, Marshall Provost has found me a place that looks suitable. He took me to see it this morning. He said he's a friend of yours. I remember you having lunch with him that day at the diner. The next step will be for you and Dr. Flowers to take a look at it."

"Any buildings on it?"

"A small ranch house with a detached garage. All flat. A couple trees for shade. A small pole building. Let's go see that hobo."

In the light of the day we could actually see the thinness of his body. Even his long dirty white hair couldn't hide the ribs and hipbones protruding.

"Did he get full this morning, Angie?"

"It took a few bowls of food but he finally quit eating." She was smiling at Charles.

"And after the first four hour interval?"

"Ate the whole amount. He's really been lapping up the water too. I'd try to get him to come but all he would do is sit just outside the reach of the branches. When I'd go inside, he'd crawl back under and curl up to sleep."

We gave Charles another bowl of food and he went out on the patio. He sat cross legged with the food near his knee. The white head popped out from under the branches.

"Hello there fella," he cooed.

The dog looked young and had the potential to be large and muscular. His eyes and nose were black. A Great Pyrenees cross, I thought. "Looks like a polar bear," I whispered from behind the curtain.

Angie giggled. "That would be a great name for him."

Charles didn't have total success by nightfall and asked if he could spend the night on the patio. It was a balmy evening. I got him a blanket, the bag of dog food and a bucket of water. By morning he and the dog were curled together between the folds of the blanket.

Chapter 25

The July Fourth Play Day was a resounding success for the Saddle Club and many of the participants had also paid their fee to participate in the trail ride later that evening. The parking lot had barely cleared before the trail riders began showing up with more trailered horses. The outing had drawn as many participants as the fall ride had. There were more new ones and most of our normal boarders.

Phil, Betty and Conner were at the fire destination. I led on Argo. Again we asked the people to partner up and I soon saw Jeremiah Johnson tipping his hat to me with a smile.

Even as I bid Jeremiah good evening, I could feel my face stiffen.

"How've you been, Madison?"

"I'm fine, thank you."

I saw Sheri on Buffalo Head Penny partner up with Shelly who brought up the rear on George.

"Phoenix is expanding already. That's quite an accomplishment."

"A testament to a fantastic barn manager, wonderful workers and horse owners."

"Have you a stall available? I'd like to board my horse here."

"I'm afraid not. In fact the new stalls were all contracted before they were completed. I would think you'd want your horse closer to you, not a whole state away."

"It would give me a reason to come more often. I'm sure not all the stalls in your wing are occupied."

"Sorry, those are for Phoenix school and show horses only."

"You could make an exception."

"No, that would open the door to trouble."

"You board Cherry Tart in your wing," he weascled.

"Arielle works for Phoenix and represents us at shows."

"I see. You'll let me know if a stall becomes available?"

"You can talk to Shelly about being put on the waiting list."

"I hear an edge in your voice, Madison. Am I pushing too hard?"

"Pushing what?"

"I told you I'd be here if Jake was no longer in the picture. I wanted to rush to your side the minute I read his obituary, but I restrained myself in consideration for you...to give you time to heal. I want to be part of your life."

"How would you have gotten hold of his obituary? I doubt he was so popular that a newspaper in the next state would have carried it."

"I have a friend who sends me all the news about Phoenix."

"And why would they do that?"

"I've an interest in it."

"Well, don't get too interested."

"No, ma'am."

The night was perfect for the music, dancing, food and laughter. Jeremiah left me alone the rest of the night. He morphed into his usual gregarious self making the outing wonderful for many wall flowers. I was pleased he was along for his ability to draw people out of themselves and toward one another.

I sought out Sheri and asked about the resolution of the horse theft episode.

"They gave him suspended jail time, a year of community service which he can do while in college, a thousand dollar fine, and ordered to stay away from me and my family."

"Will you sue for emotional compensation?"

"No. I just want him to leave us alone."

"Well, I'm glad you came tonight."

It was just after the trail ride that Charles brought Polar in for shots.

"Sorry. I thought it was important to let him relax, get used to me before bringing him in to get hurt."

Polar kept his eyes on Charles' face and behaved very well while being examined and given shots.

"So you named him Polar? Charles, thank you for taking him."

"You're welcome. The name was Angie's idea and I liked it."

I smiled to myself. Angie had broken up with her sport-watching boyfriend a month or so ago. I wondered if she had designs on Charles.

"Have we made an offer on that place?"

"Yes. We're still negotiating but I think they're going to accept our offer. The zoning is okay. Angie is helping make up advertisements and fliers announcing the opening. One of the Saddle club members, a young fella named Caden, is building donation boxes for us. I've approached a couple people about being on the board of directors along with you and Clint. Rev. Roy Dickson of the Methodist Church, Dr. Greg Bair, and Meg Shillig, a school teacher. I thought a diverse board was important. Their only common factor is they own pets and care about animals in general. Meg also suggested to a few high school boys to help get the buildings ready as community service to put on their college applications.

I felt a wave of satisfaction that I was part of the creation of this new caring facility. Charles' act of kindness to a dog that died kept rippling out to engage more and more people in the community.

The show season was still going strong. Our wins had put us in the spot light. A reporter came to interview several employees and boarders as well as Shelly and I. It increased our waiting list as well as our applications for work.

Taylor informed me that Lisa wouldn't be coming for lessons anymore. Their mom said she could quit to get ready to leave for college in the Fall.

"So she attained her goal of getting to college without any broken bones," I laughed.

"I want to thank you, Madison, for giving me the opportunity to find my direction as well."

"What's that, Taylor?"

"I've enjoyed helping Wade so much I'm going to go into education."

"That's wonderful."

"So I'll be quitting next year about midsummer."

"Are you saving lots of your earnings to put toward college?"

"Yes, ma'am. If you need me any more hours, I'm available."

"I think Dr. Flowers needs more help in the Saddle club barn, now that Charlie left."

"I'll take it. I wish we could have helped Charlie more."

"Me too. We just didn't get to him in time."

Sundays were downtime days. I allowed myself to go shopping, take in a movie or just bum about the house if I wasn't on call for the clinic. This particular Sunday I woke up and laid there thinking of Phoenix and all the people around me that felt like family. How fortunate I was. Yet, there was something missing. A special love that would put the brightness back into my life and make me feel like I belonged.

"I miss you Jake," I whispered.

I got dressed and went to the kitchen. Standing at the sink filling the coffee pot, I saw Brandi's blue and silver horse trailer in the parking lot. I went out wondering if she had found another special horse to add to our personal string. She was teaching some really advanced students that were representing Phoenix in shows.

Brandi came out of the arena and met me by the trailer.

"Hey, how was Hawaii?"

She smiled broadly. "Great. You should go sometime."

"I will someday."

"Madison, I need to ask your forgiveness. I just found out from Marshall that New Year's was supposed to be your wedding day." She took me by the elbow and guided me toward the arena. Jake had bought something for you as a wedding gift and I was going to give it to you on the October date you had originally picked to get married. But when I found out you switched and we were all in for a surprise wedding, I wanted to bring it to you right away."

My eyes were adjusting to the shadow inside the arena. I remembered Jake's words: "I'm going to get you the most fantastic wedding gift."

Before I could see him I heard a familiar nicker. My heart leaped and goose bumps formed on my arms. "Fritz?"

Thoughts swirled in my mind. Jake wanted me to have Fritz back. It WAS the most fabulous gift. And Mom...how this must have been the same kind of relationship she'd had with Gustavo. As Fritz and I stood forehead to forehead, I could sense Mom and Jake, arms linked and big smiles on their faces. Then they turned and walked away together.

When I could stop crying I noticed Fritz was already tacked up. Russ was at my side. "Leg up?"

I bent my leg and Russ hoisted me aboard. We moved out at a walk; went into a canter. The sound of his hoof beats pounded on the arena sand and echoed in my heart. I was home.